CAVE
BENEATH
the SEA

CAVE BENEATH *the* SEA

EDWARD WILLETT

Edited by Matthew Hughes
Cover and text designed by Tania Craan
Typeset by Susan Buck
Printed and bound in Canada

Library and Archives Canada Cataloguing in Publication
Willett, Edward, 1959-, author
        Cave beneath the sea / Edward Willett. ·
(The shards of Excalibur ; book 4)
Issued in print and electronic formats.
ISBN 978-1-55050-639-6 (bound).--ISBN 978-1-55050-646-4 (pdf).--
ISBN 978-1-55050-871-0 (epub).--ISBN 978-1-55050-878-9 (mobi)
        I. Title. II. Series: Willett, Edward, 1959- . Shards of Excalibur ; bk. 4.

PS8595.I5424C38 2015   jC813'.54   C2015-902922-8
                                                 C2015-902923-6

Library of Congress Control Number: 2015937034

2517 Victoria Avenue
Regina, Saskatchewan
Canada S4P 0T2
www.coteaubooks.com

10 9 8 7 6 5 4 3 2 1

Available in Canada from:
Publishers Group Canada
2440 Viking Way
Richmond, British Columbia
Canada V6V 1N2

Available in the US from:
Orca Book Publishers
www.orcabook.com
1-800-210-5277

Coteau Books gratefully acknowledges the financial support of its publishing program by: the Saskatchewan Arts Board, The Canada Council for the Arts, the Government of Saskatchewan through Creative Saskatchewan, the City of Regina. We further acknowledge the [financial] support of the Government of Canada. Nous reconnaissons l'appui [financier] du gouvernement du Canada.

Four nieces and a nephew – five books
This one is for Denae

CHAPTER ONE

SNOW DAY

Ariane Forsythe stared out the farmhouse's second-storey window at the swirling snow, and sighed. *Just my luck*, she thought. *Lady of the Lake, in freaking Saskatchewan – where lakes are frozen solid six months out of the year.*

Downstairs the radio was playing "It's Beginning to Look a Lot Like Christmas," and Aunt Phyllis was singing along, more or less in key. *Christmas*, she thought. *Christmas in two weeks, and I still don't have a clue where the fourth shard of Excalibur is.*

It wasn't supposed to have worked out like this. When she had first transported Aunt Phyllis and her aunt's old friend Emma Macphail to the Barringer Historic Farm Bed and Breakfast (and as she'd suggested to Wally, they'd both proved to be remarkably composed about being dissolved into water and whisked across the province in incorporeal form), she'd thought she'd be certain to sense the location of the fourth shard within a day or two. She'd expected to transport herself there easily, grab it, and return, and then go on to find the fifth and final piece, the hilt, within another week or so. With that much of the sword she could apparently (at least she'd been told she'd be able to) force Merlin – now living in the modern world as cybernetics billionaire Rex Major – to give up the piece he had, and that would have been that. Door to Faerie closed, Rex Major reduced to an ordinary man, no more magic, no more Lady of the Lake, back to school, back to her poor cat Pendragon, now living with the lady next door in Regina, back to the ordinary concerns of ordinary fifteen-year-old girls.

Such as finding her mother. With Rex Major no longer a threat, with the power of the Lady vanished from the world, there'd be no reason for her mother to keep running and hiding – if that was what she was doing. Their only lead was a photo from a convenience store in Carlyle. There was no reason to think her mom was still anywhere near that town, or even in Saskatchewan, but at least it was a place to start.

But she'd sensed nothing. The "few days" at Barringer Farm had stretched to two weeks, then three. And now to six.

On December 2 they'd celebrated Wally's fifteenth birthday. "Now we're the same age!" he'd said gleefully to Ariane.

"Only until March 12," she said. "Then I'll be sweet sixteen and you'll still be a runty fifteen-year-old."

He'd stuck out his tongue at her.

Two more weeks had gone by. Now Christmas was coming, the goose was getting fat, and here in a farmhouse Ariane sat.

Sam and Nancy Barringer, the proprietors of the B&B, had greeted Aunt Phyllis like a long-lost cousin. Apparently they'd hit it off big-time during her previous stay at the farm – so much so that, after a week, Sam and Nancy and Phyllis and Emma had somehow decided that Phyllis and Emma would housesit while Sam and Nancy went off to spend an indeterminate number of wintry weeks with their daughter in New Mexico, something they'd always wanted to do but had never been able to take time for.

It had all worked out perfectly. Phyllis and Emma and Ariane and Wally, tucked away in a rustic farmhouse on the northern slopes of the Cypress Hills, their only link to the outside world a land-line telephone, were as hidden from Rex Major's Internet-surfing magic as they could possibly be. Wonderful.

Except for the little fact that Ariane didn't have a clue what to do next.

She looked down from the swirling snow to the sheet of paper in front of her. Aunt Phyllis had formally withdrawn her from Oscana Collegiate in Regina, but that didn't mean she was off the books-hook. It turned out Aunt Phyllis's old friend Emma was a retired schoolteacher. It had also turned out that the "interesting books" Aunt Phyllis had mentioned seeing in the parlour during her previous visit to Barringer Farm included a number of schoolbooks and classics of English literature. Which was why Ariane was now trying to write an essay about Agnes Macphail, the first woman elected to Canada's Parliament and apparently a distant relation of Emma's. She'd gotten as far as "Agnes Macphail began her career as a country schoolteacher." She'd written that twenty minutes ago.

She sighed and put down the pen, then shoved her chair back from the desk, stood up, and stretched. It was almost time to fetch Wally.

Doing schoolwork without Internet access was a struggle for Ariane, but Wally clearly felt as if he'd had a part of himself amputated. Not only that, their only hope for tracking down Ariane's mother was to troll the Web for traces. There was no doubt that was what Rex Major would be doing. Of course, as one of the richest men in the world, he could also hire an army of private investigators, and possibly had.

There was another problem, too. Major had talked Wally's parents – well, magically Commanded them, actually – into letting Wally withdraw from school and live with him, but that arrangement had been permanently shattered when Wally had fled Major's Toronto penthouse (clobbering a security guard with a poker in the process), gotten himself to Prince Albert, rescued Aunt Phyllis, stolen a sizeable amount of money from Major, flown to New Zealand on his own, and actually found and retrieved the third shard of Excalibur before either Ariane or Merlin had gotten their hands on it.

Major's response had been to turn his attention to Wally's sister Felicia, a.k.a. "Flish." Being of the same family, she shared Wally's mystical connection to their distant ancestor, the one and only King Arthur, and thus would apparently serve Major's nefarious purposes just as well. With Felicia now occupying Wally's former place in the lap of penthouse luxury on the north shore of Lake Ontario, Major had had no reason to continue to Command Wally's parents to, basically, forget about their son. Instead, he'd told them that Wally had run away in Toronto.

Ordinarily, a single runaway wouldn't have made the news, but once police traced Wally first to Prince Albert, then to Saskatoon, and then to New Zealand, his disappearance had become a national story – especially when they uncovered the fact that he'd never used his return ticket, and the last person to see him had been the taxi driver who had taken him to the base of the hiking trail leading to Lake Putahi, where the third shard of Excalibur lay hidden on an island.

A massive search-and-rescue effort had been launched in New Zealand, not surprisingly to no avail, since Wally was safe in Saskatchewan the whole time. The story had finally died away a month ago, with the working theory being that Wally had gotten lost in the mountains of New

Zealand and met an unfortunate fate. But since that hadn't been confirmed, Wally's photo was in police missing-persons databases all over Canada.

Oddly enough, Rex Major's name had never surfaced in the media as the person Wally had run away *from. The Voice of Command at work,* Ariane thought. It was peculiar that both Wally and Flish were immune to Major's power to Command, although their father, Jim, wasn't. Ariane and Wally had discussed it and decided it must be the work of the sword. A semi-sentient magical entity, it had apparently decided that it would be in its own interest for the two latest-generation descendants of King Arthur to be protected from outside influences – except, of course, from the influence wielded by Excalibur itself.

Ariane's and Wally's problem had been to find a way to get Wally Internet access without Rex Major detecting him, or, if he did spot Wally, without being able to find him. Wally had pointed out the best way to do that was to access the Web from multiple, widely separated, randomly chosen locations. But Wally obviously couldn't fly commercially without getting caught in either Merlin's magical-software net or by the standard screening procedures, so all travel arrangements had to be courtesy of the Ariane Travel Agency: "The Lady of the Lake, for when you absolutely, positively, have to arrive at your destination soaking wet," Wally had quipped.

Which was why Wally was currently in Gravenhurst, Ontario, "Gateway to Muskoka," using a public computer in the local library, digging through online newspapers, police reports, photos, and everything else he could think of, looking for some trace of Emily Forsythe, Ariane's mother.

But the afternoon was getting on (and of course it was already an hour later in Gravenhurst), and the only way Wally could get home was for Ariane to go get him, so it was time to get moving.

She took another look at the snow falling outside, thickening by the minute. She felt a sudden pang of worry. The farmhouse might be safe, but it was also a prison. The farmhouse water came from a well, and the aquifer it drew from didn't extend far enough for her to use it as a pathway to anywhere else. She could travel through the clouds, but not in heavy snow. She could wield frozen water as a weapon, but couldn't travel through it. So the falling snow acted as a barrier, keeping her grounded.

She could get to Wally from Maple Creek, thirty kilometres away, courtesy of any tap in any bathroom or kitchen. But she couldn't bring him back there. She could only materialize them in a body of water deep enough to submerge them, and while Maple Creek had a swimming pool, it was an outdoor pool, snow-drifted and forlorn this time of year. Elkwater, the other relatively nearby settlement, had a resort hotel with a pool; but it was a saltwater pool, useless to Ariane.

That meant the only place they could reliably return to after each of Wally's jaunts in search of Internet access was Medicine Hat, more than an hour's drive from Barringer Farm in good weather. And the way this storm was shaping up...

Ariane grabbed the backpack she always kept handy, the one that held her bathing suit, a towel, a change of clothes, a waterproof flashlight and a knife. She already wore the first shard of Excalibur strapped to her side beneath a tensor bandage: she only took it off when she was showering or sleeping. She grabbed her coat from the foot of the big four-poster bed and hurried out into the upstairs hall. Six rooms opened onto it, and a central staircase led down from a well in the middle. The whole house glowed with polished wood and antique glass and brass. It was like living in a Lucy Maud Montgomery novel.

She thumped down the stairs. The radio had moved on to "Rockin' Around the Christmas Tree," but Aunt Phyllis wasn't singing. Instead she stood in the big kitchen, with its oak cabinetry and black-and-white-tiled floor, one hand pulling back the chintz curtains that hung over the white enamel sink, peering out into the yard. She turned to Ariane, worry plain on her face. "Oh, dear," she said. "I didn't realize it had gotten so bad."

"We'd better go," Ariane said. "Before it gets worse."

"Emma had best drive you," Aunt Phyllis said. "You know I don't like driving in snow. She grew up on a farm and learned to drive when she was thirteen."

Ariane blinked at that. Emma Macphail had surprised her pretty much every day since she'd met her. "Okay," she said. "Where is she?"

"Here," Emma said, coming into the kitchen from the dining room. Tall, thin, and gaunt, with a shock of unruly white hair, she cut a striking figure. Ariane doubted she'd ever had the slightest problem with classroom discipline when she'd been teaching full time: she must have been terrifying.

Emma already had her coat on and held her gloves in her left hand, the keys to the Barringers' ten-year-old Ford Explorer in the other. "I'm sorry, Ariane, I was engrossed in my book and wasn't watching the weather. You're quite right, we should hurry." She smiled at Aunt Phyllis. "If worst comes to worst, we'll just stay at the hotel tonight. I'll call."

Ariane zipped up her coat and jammed a tuque on her head. She pulled open the kitchen door and stepped into the small back porch, where she extracted her boots from the pile by the door, then sat down on the wooden bench that spanned one wall of the porch to tug them on. Emma sat beside her to pull on her own practical zip-up boots. Then she opened the back door.

An icy blast of freezing air and wind-blown snow instantly dropped the porch temperature twenty degrees. "Can we get through this?" Ariane said uneasily.

"Can't tell from here," Emma said. "There's not much snow on the ground yet, so hopefully the drifts aren't too bad. Come on." She led the way out into the storm.

The Barringer Historic Farm Bed and Breakfast stood atop a hill, with a long drive leading up to it past the barn. Sam and Nancy had long since stopped farming the land themselves, instead renting it out to Jimmy Ferguson, the next-door neighbour who also looked after the snow-plowing and shovelling and general upkeep. The barn doubled as the garage, but the Explorer had been left out that morning in anticipation of this afternoon's trip to Medicine Hat. A thick white blanket covered it, thicker on the lee side, where the wind hadn't blown it away.

Emma and Ariane trudged through the snow to the vehicle. Ariane grabbed the snowbrush and began clearing the Explorer's windows while Emma cranked the engine. It started without difficulty – despite the snow, it wasn't particularly cold, around minus-ten degrees Celsius or so – and Ariane climbed inside. "Good day for four-wheel drive," Emma said cheerfully as she backed up and turned so they were pointing down the long winding road that led to the grid road that led to Saskatchewan 724, which turned into Alberta 515, which led to the Buffalo Trail, which led to the TransCanada Highway, which led to Medicine Hat. The trip took an hour in good weather.

This wasn't good weather.

Still, it was early in the winter and, as Emma had noted, there hadn't been a lot of snow yet. As Ariane had hoped, the roads weren't drifting closed, at least not yet, and although she could see only a couple of hundred metres ahead, the road was still mostly brown and not white, so Emma was unlikely to drive into the ditch. And they still had a couple of hours of daylight. But coming back...

"I think we probably *will* need to stay the night in Medicine Hat," Emma said, echoing Ariane's unspoken concern. "If it's still storming we won't want to try to drive back in the dark."

"That means a computer check-in," Ariane said uneasily.

"In my name," Emma said. "It shouldn't raise any red flags. Rex Major hasn't connected me to you lot."

That we know of, Ariane thought. But there was no point in telling Emma that; she knew it as well as Ariane. Besides, risks were everywhere. Driving into the ditch and possibly freezing to death by the side of the road in the middle of nowhere was probably a greater one than the possibility that Major would connect a random check-in at the Medicine Hat Lodge to his young adversaries.

Probably.

They turned north onto the Buffalo Trail about an hour after leaving the farm. Visibility improved a bit, and they made better time driving north to the TransCanada. Once they were on the four-lane, the storm seemed barely a nuisance. But they'd lost a lot of time nonetheless, and Ariane was uneasily aware that the appointed hour when she was supposed to retrieve Wally from Gravenhurst – 6 p.m., his time – had come and gone, and was receding further into the past with every second.

Ariane and Wally had the challenging process of travelling by swimming pool down to a science. Every time Wally went on one of his research trips, they would drive into Medicine Hat (after calling the Lodge first to make sure that there was public swimming that day – sometimes, when the hotel was full, drop-in swimming wasn't available). They went into their respective change rooms and put on swimsuits, leaving their clothes in the locker. (Ariane had made a point of buying a new one-piece to replace the bikini she'd stolen from Flish's wardrobe. It hadn't covered nearly as much of her as she liked to have covered.)

They didn't actually vanish from the pool itself; they didn't need to. Instead they just waited until one of the bathrooms was empty and no one was watching, and slipped in together. Ariane turned on the tap, and away they went.

She'd become much better at navigating: she could pick a town on the map and find her way unerringly to it, through senses she couldn't describe, even to herself, especially since those abilities only existed when she was in the magical watery form the powers she'd inherited from the Lady of the Lake permitted her to take. When she materialized again, everything she had done in that immaterial state seemed almost dream-like.

They'd chosen Gravenhurst for this latest trip because, like the other towns Wally had travelled to in order to access the Internet, it had an indoor pool. In the case of Gravenhurst, the pool belonged to the YMCA, and offered recreational adult swimming in the morning. (They'd researched it at the Maple Creek library: they weren't worried – much – about Rex Major connecting a search for swimming pools to the pair of them.)

She'd taken Wally to Gravenhurst early that morning, the two of them materializing in the YMCA pool and swimming up from the bottom of the deep end, startling two elderly ladies gently exercising in the shallow portion. "Where'd you two come from?" one had said, laughing. "You startled us!"

"And why are you carrying a backpack in the pool?" the other had asked Wally.

"Long story," Wally had said cheerfully.

"Sorry for startling you," Ariane added. "Come on, Wally."

She'd given up worrying about explaining anything to

anyone when they were seen arriving in a new location. People would make up their own explanations, none of which, she was pretty sure, would involve the Lady of the Lake, Excalibur, or magical powers.

They'd walked, dripping, out of sight, Ariane had ordered them both dry, and then Wally had trotted off to the change room while Ariane had gone into a washroom, turned on the tap, and headed back to Medicine Hat.

Sometimes Ariane just waited in Medicine Hat until it was time to retrieve Wally, but that morning Ariane had asked Emma to take her back to the farm so she could work on her homework. Considering she'd only managed one sentence of her essay, that had clearly been a waste of time. Ariane stared out the window at the snowy landscape. *And now we're late.*

Emma turned off of the TransCanada at the first exit into Medicine Hat. The Medicine Hat Lodge, a four-storey building of brown brick, stood close by the highway, and two minutes later they pulled to a stop in its parking lot.

The snow had thickened in just the last few minutes of the drive. Emma sighed as she turned off the engine. "Looks like we're definitely spending the night," she said. "I'll book a couple of rooms – one for you and me and one for Wally."

Ariane nodded. She hurried into the lobby, filled with the fading light of the snowy day outside through the big slanting atrium windows overhead. Emma followed at a more sedate space. "You check in, Aunt Emma," she said loudly for the benefit of the desk clerk. "I'm going swimming!"

She heard the clerk, a young First Nations woman, laugh. "She's excited," she said.

"She loves the water," Emma said.

"So do I," the clerk said.

Not like I do, Ariane thought.

The pool area featured a leisure pool and a four-storey dual waterslide. It was quiet that evening. The worst thing from Ariane's point of view was that the waterpark filled an interior courtyard, so that hotel room windows stared down at it from all directions. But who really noticed an extra kid or two in a pool? She and Wally always materialized at the bottom of the waterslide, and her powers, more finely tuned all the time, allowed her to delay until the area was empty. Who would note that the two youngsters climbing out had never actually gone down the slide?

Into the change room, out of her clothes, into her swimsuit, leaving the shard of Excalibur in its place, snug against her side. She put on the backpack and went over to the change-room sinks: no need to go into the pool to *start* her trip. She turned on the water. Just before she touched it, she checked the time on the wall clock.

Seven o'clock. Eight o'clock in Ontario. She was two hours late.

Sorry, Wally, she thought uneasily, then let the water take her away.

CHAPTER TWO

A FACE IN THE CROWD

WALLY SAT BACK in his chair in front of one of the computer terminals in the Gravenhurst Public Library and
stretched, reaching up toward the fluorescent lights overhead. Outside the narrow windows, rain fell from a grey
sky, already darkening toward twilight. On the desk in
front of him the monitor glowed cold white, like the snow
back in Saskatchewan. And just like the wintry fields
around Barringer Farm, the monitor was currently barren.

Another day wasted, Wally thought. *The trouble is, I'm
a couple of years too early.*

What he really needed was a search engine that could
take a face from a photo and then find, not just copies of
that same photo – that part was easy – but that face in
the background of photos taken by other people. CSIS –
the Canadian Security Intelligence Service – might have
the capability, but the public search engines just weren't
there yet.

Still, he kept hoping. He'd tried every image-search engine he could think of in the half-dozen times he'd made
one of these bizarre swish-through-the-water-and-emerge-
in-a-strange-swimming-pool trips to some random town

with a library. On his first trip he'd visited a copy shop and scanned the old photo of her mom Ariane had provided. Now he carried it around on a USB stick in his pocket, plugging it into computer after computer. So far, nothing.

Every other search he could think of had turned up empty as well. Emily Forsythe was out there somewhere – they knew that, because Wally had seen a blurry photograph captured from some convenience store camera in Carlyle, Saskatchewan, weeks ago when he'd briefly been an honoured guest of Rex Major's instead of a mortal enemy. His sister, Flish, now occupied the luxurious guest room that had been his in Major's Toronto lakeshore condo and she was undoubtedly also enjoying the theatre room.

He sighed. He missed that giant screen.

He glanced at his watch, a brand-new waterproof-to-two-hundred-metres diving watch he'd bought with some of the money he'd purloined from Rex Major. Ariane would be showing up in the pool in less than an hour. Time to call it quits.

He lowered his gaze to the terminal – and froze.

He'd thought the latest search, using a brand-new still-in-beta engine he'd stumbled across while poking through some of the stranger corners of the Internet, had simply hung up: he'd entered the image and the screen had frozen. But it had suddenly come back to life.

The search engine showed two hits. The first was a link to the *North Shore News*, a newspaper serving West Vancouver, B.C. He clicked on the link.

A photo appeared: a group of people eating outside a restaurant with a green awning, Canadian and B.C. flags flying, and a big sign spelling out, in lower-case letters, "troll's."

Wally knew the place: he'd had fish and chips there one

summer when he was nine, while his family waited in Horseshoe Bay to board the ferry to Vancouver Island. He leaned in closer.

The search engine had placed a box around one slightly out-of-focus face. Fuzzy though it was, there could be no doubt: it was Emily Forsythe.

Ariane's mother.

Wally checked the date. The photo had been taken a month earlier.

His initial surge of excitement faded. She'd probably just been waiting for a ferry. She could be anywhere by now.

But there was a second link. He clicked it.

This one took him to someone's Facebook page, and a selfie: a young Asian woman smiling at the camera she was clearly holding out at arm's length. Out of focus in the background was a B.C. Ferry docked at the Horseshoe Bay terminal. But just a few steps behind the young woman, turned toward the camera, much clearer than in the previous photo, he saw Emily Forsythe.

And that photo had been taken just two weeks ago.

If she was there for two weeks, Wally thought, *she's probably still there. That's where she's gone to ground!*

He quickly highlighted and copied the URLs for the two photos, pasted them into a word processing document, and saved them them on the USB stick. Then he pulled out the stick and stood up from the workstation. He got his backpack out from under the chair and headed for the library's glass front doors.

A man stood there, holding the door open, a big black man in a black suit, talking to someone outside on the rain-pounded sidewalk.

Wally felt as though he'd been slugged in the stomach. He ducked behind a bookshelf, heart pounding.

It can't be.

He peered around the corner of the shelf, then jerked his head back again.

It is.

Emeka. One of Rex Major's bodyguards.

But there's no way, Wally thought. *There's no way he could have found me. Major couldn't have known we were coming here. He couldn't have...*

Unless...

He felt sick. They'd searched for swimming pools near libraries over and over. This was the fifth town he'd been to. And somehow, that combination of search terms had flagged something on the Internet, somewhere in some server running Rex Major's Excalibur Computer Systems software, the software that contained tendrils of Merlin's magic – magic that was growing stronger as more shards of Excalibur surfaced.

Major had seen that the latest search had turned up Gravenhurst, and had taken a chance. He'd sent Emeka on the two-hour trip from Toronto, just on the long-shot possibility Wally or Ariane, or both, would turn up. He'd lucked out, while Wally's luck had *run* out.

I'm trapped, Wally thought; and then, fiercely, *No. There has to be a back door.*

He headed away from the front door, but after six steps he stopped, swearing silently at himself.

He hadn't cleared the browser. The picture of Emily's mother would still be showing.

He hurried over to the computer stations, cleared the browser's search history, closed the browser, straightened up –

And found himself staring at Emeka, who stared back, eyes wide. Clearly he'd never *really* expected to find Wally in a library in Gravenhurst.

Wally took advantage of the big man's momentary confusion to dash past him.

"Stop!" Emeka shouted as Wally charged to the door. "Thief!" he added for good measure.

Not very original, Wally thought. But it didn't matter: another big man in a black suit loomed in the main door. Wally changed direction and charged back into the library. Librarians shouted at him. A couple of small children goggled at him wide-eyed. And Emeka raced after him, banging into a kid-size chair and sending it tumbling across the room. Wally heard him swear. *Not in front of the kids, Emeka*, he thought.

Every library he'd ever been in had a door marked "Staff Only" at the back, and the Gravenhurst Public Library was no exception. He burst through the forbidden portal, dashed through a workspace as two more librarians yelled at him, slammed open another door, found himself in a short corridor, and a moment later burst out the back door of the library into the parking lot, surrounded by mounds of recent snow melting fast under the unseasonable December rain. *Lucky it's not freezing rain*, Wally thought fleetingly – that would have certainly slowed him down. Instead, it was just really, really *cold* rain.

Instead of crossing the parking lot, he turned the corner and ran down the gravel-covered alley behind·the library, splashing through puddles and slush. He dashed through someone's back yard and down their front sidewalk, across the street, between two more houses, zigged and zagged several more blocks, and eventually, panting, soaked to the skin, freezing cold, and unable to run another step, found himself in a gravelled parking lot, staring at a sign that read, bilingually, "Fisheries and Oceans, Small Craft Harbours, Gull Lake (Gravenhurst), Managed by the Town of Gravenhurst."

Beyond the sign stretched a half-frozen lake, the woods and rocks of the far shore dim grey shadows in the rain, the water puddling on the ice near the shore.

We should have picked a town near a lake that doesn't freeze in the winter, Wally thought. *But who wants to materialize in a freezing cold lake, even if you can just wish yourself dry?*

So instead, they'd focussed on swimming pools. And clearly, it was the search for swimming pools that had caused Rex Major to send Emeka out here. He looked back up the street. He seemed to have lost the big black man, at least for the moment – but if Wally's guess was correct, Emeka knew he would be heading to the swimming pool. He'd probably already gone that way himself.

Which meant he'd be waiting for Ariane.

Wally sighed, took a deep breath, and started running again. He was going to freeze to death if he stood still much longer anyway.

The Gravenhurst YMCA was about a kilometre away. Wally ran toward it along the lakefront, passing houses surrounded by half-melted snowdrifts, eventually turning left to cross the railroad tracks. Just past the tracks, a sidewalk angled through an opening in a chain-link fence toward the main entrance of the YMCA, a low-rise, modern building of steel and glass. Wally slowed and peered through the rain, looking for either of the men who had surprised him at the library. Emeka, big enough to play centre for the Saskatchewan Roughriders, seemed an unlikely candidate for stealthy lurking. The trouble was, he'd only caught a glimpse of the other guy, and aside from the fact he'd been wearing a dark suit – the *de rigeur* uniform of Rex Major's hired thugs, it seemed – his appearance had made no impression on Wally. *That's probably why they all wear the same thing. Like in* Men in Black. *Who notices another guy in a dark suit?*

Still, the slush-streaked grounds of the building seemed devoid of life – not too surprising in the cold downpour. Now that he'd quit running, Wally was beginning to shiver again. He wished he had Ariane's power to order the water off his body.

He wished he had Ariane.

They can't grab me from the lobby of the YMCA, he thought.

He started down the sidewalk.

Four pine trees grew to the left of the sidewalk, three too small to hide anyone larger than Wally – and one more substantial tree, from behind which Emeka abruptly emerged. Wally stopped dead.

"Hello, Wally," the big man said, his voice deep enough to qualify as a growl. "Mr. Major would like to talk to you."

"The feeling is very much not mutual," Wally said. He looked behind him. A black SUV – didn't Major's men ever drive anything else? – had just pulled up at the opening through the chain-link fence. The other man he'd seen at the library got out.

Wally had always thought swearing was a sign of a poor vocabulary, but he lowered his standards with a single muttered word, then turned right and ran across the soaking grass toward another opening in the fence, just below a big sign headed "Centennial Centre." Below the title temporary lettering read "Join the YMCA Running Club Today!"

I think I just did, Wally thought.

The second man from the SUV charged along the fence to head him off. Emeka pounded at his heels. Across the street Colonel Sanders watched the chase from the sign of a Kentucky Fried Chicken franchise, but if anyone looking out wondered why two men were chasing a boy they didn't bother coming out into the rain to find out.

Wally skirted the little slush-choked skateboard park adjacent to the YMCA and angled away from the fence, which ended at a line of trees and shrubs. He plunged in among the bushes and, momentarily out of his pursuers' sight, immediately changed his trajectory, hurtling a sad grey snowdrift to avoid leaving tracks, racing through someone's backyard, changing direction again on the far side of the house, running through another yard, altering direction again, scrambling over a fence, and finally emerging, heart pounding, breath coming in wet gasps, onto another street. He changed directions yet again, splashed through more puddles and slush, left the houses behind, and finally emerged onto a street lined with small businesses. Up ahead, he spotted a department store. *Perfect.* He looked back – no pursuers in sight. He dashed into the store and stopped, chest heaving, dripping water as the clerk behind the front counter, a girl two or three years older than he was, looked up from a copy of *Teen Vogue* and gave him a surprised look. "Wet out there," he said, trying to sound nonchalant. "Did you know *Mythbusters* proved you get less wet running than you do walking?" He shook his head, spraying water from his shaggy red hair. "Can't say it worked for me."

"Uh-huh," the girl said, and went back to her magazine.

Wally looked around the deserted store, and then out the window at the equally deserted street. *Guess I lost them. But now what?*

They'd return to the Y, of course. They knew – or guessed – that was where Ariane would make an appearance. They couldn't do anything to her – not on a rainy day – but they could still hope to grab *him*, and if Rex Major had shown one thing over the past couple of months, it was that he thought hostage-taking was a *great* way to get Ariane to do what he wanted.

Trouble was, he was right. Ariane had given up a shard in the Northwest Territories when Major had threatened Wally's life. Afterward, Ariane and Wally had stolen it back, but the example had been set. Ariane had actually *led* Major to the third shard, in New Zealand, because he'd taken Aunt Phyllis captive. Only the fact Wally had managed to free Aunt Phyllis and get to New Zealand to let Ariane know about it had saved the shard that time.

Major clearly thought Ariane would give up both of the shards she had if he could grab Wally again, but today's attack was just a spur-of-the-moment attempt: they all knew, Ariane and Wally and Major alike, that the ultimate hostage-taking prize was Ariane's missing mother. Major knew she was alive, and knew Ariane would do anything to protect her. He was searching for her just as Wally had been. And he couldn't be far behind. He had access to computer algorithms Wally could only dream about. He might have already seen the Horseshoe Bay photos. He might have already sent men to B.C. to try to find her.

He might already *have* her.

No, Wally thought. *If he did, Emeka wouldn't be here in Gravenhurst. If Major had Ariane's mom, he wouldn't bother chasing me. But we still have to act fast. We have to get out to B.C. and find Ariane's mom before Major can.*

But first, we have to get out of this trap.

Ariane could show up at the YMCA at any moment. Wally had to get back there, but he had to get back there without being caught.

He looked around the store, and felt like a cartoon character above whose head a light bulb had just illuminated. *Department store...clothes!*

He'd stolen quite a lot of money from Rex Major's bank account during the brief time he'd had access to it, and thus it was courtesy of Rex Major that he always carried a lot of cash with him when he came on these research jaunts, just in case. In case of what, he'd never been sure, but he thought he'd just figured it out.

"Where's your boys' clothing section?" he asked the girl.

She pointed, and Wally set off deeper into the store.

He had been wearing blue jeans, white socks, red Converse sneakers and a down-filled jacket over a T-shirt that read, "You don't have to tell *me* winter is coming, I'm from Saskatchewan." But within a few minutes all of that, sopping wet though it was, was jammed into his backpack, and he was decked out in brown khakis, a green sweater over a white golf shirt, brown suede shoes over black socks, and a blue windbreaker. He'd jammed his red hair up into a weird cap that looked like a failed knitting experiment, and added dark-lensed black-rimmed sunglasses. He didn't look a bit like himself.

He hoped.

A couple of other customers had come in while he was changing; he stood in line behind them at the till. When it was his turn, the girl's eyebrows raised.

"Don't ask," Wally said. "Parental orders."

The girl nodded, understanding (false though it was) dawning in her blue eyes. "Parents. No living with them sometimes."

"My parents can't even live with each other," Wally said.

"I hear you," the girl replied.

As she rang up the total from the bar-coded tags he'd already pulled from his new purchases, Wally had to swallow a lump in his throat. He felt bad about his parents. He kind of relished the idea of all the people who had teased and bullied him over the years suddenly discovering he was way cooler than they were – because what could be cooler than escaping Saskatchewan all the way to New Zealand and then disappearing under mysterious circumstances? – but he hated the thought of his parents believing him dead. Sure, they had split up, and maybe they'd mostly been too busy and self-involved over the past few years to pay much attention to him, but he was sure they loved him in *some* fashion. He didn't like to think of them hurting.

But he and Ariane had talked about it, and they'd agreed there was no safe way to let his parents know he was okay, not without the risk of exposing his whereabouts. Being found by Major's men here in Gravenhurst (or anywhere else) didn't really count: if he and Ariane could just meet up, she could whisk them away in an instant and once again Major would have no idea where they were.

He hoped.

He paid in cash, took his change, hefted his backpack, and went to the door of the department store. The rain had slackened, though it hadn't stopped altogether, and any improvement in visibility was more than countered by the fact it was getting dark.

Wally pulled on his backpack and set off in the rain for the YMCA. Ariane should be arriving there any minute.

CHAPTER THREE

THE BATTLE AT THE YMCA

ARIANE EMERGED INTO THE DEEP END of an empty pool sparsely lit by silvery circular light fixtures high above in a wooden ceiling, with only night showing beyond the big rain-spattered windows. Above her loomed a high-diving board.

Among the ways in which her magical gift had evolved since she'd first inherited it from the Lady was the ability to sense the contents of the body of water in which she was about to materialize. She'd always been able to do that when she *touched* a body of water – she knew exactly where the discarded grocery carts and beer bottles lurked in Regina's Wascana Lake, for instance – but only since she'd had two shards of Excalibur in her possession had she begun to develop the ability to do so in advance.

It had proved helpful several times since she'd begun spiriting Wally to various places to conduct Internet re-search. She could hold off resuming bodily form until she was certain there was no one else in the pool.

The Gravenhurst YMCA actually had *two* pools: the lap pool in which she had just materialized, and a leisure pool. On this Friday night, at just after 8 p.m. local time, open adult swimming was going on, but apparently not much of it; she couldn't hear any voices from the leisure pool, out of sight from the lap pool around a corner.

High above, fluorescent light glimmered behind glass windows overlooking the pool – a program room of some sort. Ariane had no idea what might be going on in there. She just hoped nobody had seen her mysterious appearance. Although, really, how would they react? Clearly she was a very real teenage girl in a swimsuit, just like countless others who must use this pool, so she couldn't really have simply popped into existence out of nowhere, no matter what it had looked like, no matter how odd the fact she had a backpack in the pool with her. They'd just assume they'd somehow missed her through the reflection of the lights on the water, or if they were old enough, they might think they had suffered a mini-stroke.

Ariane smiled at the thought as she tossed the backpack onto the concrete apron surrounding the pool and clambered out after it. She ordered the water off the backpack, but left her body wet in case she ran into anyone when she –

"Where'd you come from?" said a voice.

Ariane jumped, and turned to see a girl about her own age, wearing a sporty black one-piece, at the corner leading around to the leisure pool.

"Just swimming a few laps," Ariane said.

The girl laughed. "They must have been awfully quick ones. I just stepped around the corner for a second, and you weren't here when I left."

"I'm easy to overlook," Ariane said. She kept her voice light. *No more questions*, she thought. "Well, all done here. Have a good swim."

"Wait," the other girl said. Ariane tensed. The water in the pool swirled uneasily, responding to her sudden pang of fear.

Stop it! she ordered herself. *She's not a threat. She's just curious.*

The girl glanced at the pool. "Weird," she said. Then she turned back to Ariane. "But you want to know something even weirder? I don't know you, but I've got a message for you."

"A message?" The water in the pool swirled again. Could she be one of Rex Major's...?

"From a boy." The girl's face crinkled into a smile. "A skinny red-headed boy with freckles."

Wally? "My...brother?" she said tentatively, because she didn't know if that was what Wally had called himself.

"Guess so," the girl said. "He was hanging around in the rain out on the street. He said to tell you..." She laughed. "This sounds so crazy. I feel like I'm in a bad spy movie."

"Tell me what?" Ariane said. The water gurgled and heaped itself up in little wavelets, drawing the girl's attention again.

"I think the pool needs work," she said, frowning at it.

"What did he say to tell me?"

The girl looked back at her, now appearing a little offended. "No need to get snippy. I'm doing you a favour."

"Sorry," Ariane said. The water bubbled. "*Sorry*. It's just...I was expecting to meet him here. And I'm late. So I need to hear what he had to say."

The other girl shrugged. "He said he can't get in here because RM has men watching the Y. Whatever that means."

What? Ariane groaned inwardly. And she was two hours late. Two hours! Anything might have happened to him. "How long ago was this?"

"Hmmm...forty-five minutes, maybe?"

"Did he say where he was going?" *Surely he's not still standing out in the rain...*

"KFC," the girl said. "Across the street." She was frowning down at Ariane's swimsuit, where the shard of Excalibur strapped to her skin made a noticeable bump. "What's that thing on your side?"

"Insulin injector," Ariane said. "Thank you for your help." She brushed past the girl and headed toward the change rooms.

"You're welcome!" the girl called after her. Then, "Oh, good, the pool's back to normal."

Ariane pulled her black jeans and black T-shirt on over her now bone-dry swimsuit and tugged on white running shoes over her bare feet, but she hesitated before leaving the change room. If "RM" had men watching the "Y," they were expecting her. How could she evade them?

And then, suddenly, she didn't care. *If they're watching,* she thought grimly, *they're not going to be lurking in the lobby looking to waylay me, not in full view of the front desk staff. They'll be outside. In the rain. Surrounded by water.*

Where I am literally in my element.

She shouldered her backpack and walked out into the long, high-ceilinged corridor that ran the length of the building, striding boldly past the front desk to the glass street doors. She pushed them open and stepped out under the portico that sheltered the entrance.

The first thing she saw was that the rain had turned to snow, big, fluffy flakes spiraling down in the light that spilled out under the portico. *Great,* she thought. *No using the rain.*

But plenty of water still puddled the ground, glimmering in the lights from the building and street. Lots to work with if Major's men tried anything. She squared her shoulders and strode boldly into the darkness. The red-and-white glow of the KFC outlet shone through the snow to her left, just the other side of a fence and a road. She headed that way.

The black SUV came out of nowhere, lights off. It blocked the opening through the chain-link fence onto the street. She stopped as the driver door opened. A man came around the front of the vehicle, indistinct in the snow and darkness. She tensed, ready to pull water to her and use it to –

A big arm wrapped across her chest from behind. She barely had time to gasp before a dark-skinned hand came up and clamped a cloth over her nose and mouth. A pungent, sweetish smell filled her nostrils. Roaring filled her ears. She tried to reach for the water all around her, but she couldn't concentrate. The shard strapped to her side blazed with power, but with her brain reeling, she couldn't draw from it. She sagged, consciousness fading...

"Leave her alone!" The shout seemed to come from far away. Someone cried out, there was the sound of a scuffle, a splashing thud. Whoever had hold of Ariane suddenly released her. She fell to her hands and knees, gasping for air, the world whirling around her, and raised her head to try to see what was going on through eyes that didn't want to focus.

Wally faced the man who'd grabbed Ariane, a broken tree branch held in one hand like a sword. Behind him a second man lay curled on the ground, hands between his legs, moaning. The one who'd had hold of Ariane, a big black man built like a football player, laughed, the sound deep and scornful. "You going to face me with nothing more than a stick, little boy?"

"It was all I needed for your friend," Wally panted.

"But I am not my friend," the black man said. And attacked. Moving faster than Ariane would have thought someone that size *could* move, he lunged, trying to grab the branch from Wally.

But Wally wasn't there. Ariane gasped as she sensed

power flowing from the shard of Excalibur at her side, not *to* her, but *away* from her: to Wally.

And Wally, with contemptuous, fluid ease, ducked under the outstretched hands, spun, and slammed the branch into the back of the big man's knees. The man slammed to the ground, grunting, as his legs collapsed. Wally spun again and brought the stick down on his attacker's head. The man groaned, tried to lift himself, and then collapsed. It was hard to be sure in the dim and uncertain light, but Ariane thought she saw blood pooling on the concrete.

Wally threw the branch aside. "What are you wearing?" Ariane said muzzily as he helped her to his feet. "You weren't wearing that this morning."

"We can discuss my wardrobe later," he said. "Get us out of here."

Ariane reached for the power, reached for the water – and couldn't connect. "Can't," she said. "Not yet." She coughed. Her throat felt raw. "They tried to knock me out with something...chloroform, I think. My brain's...not working yet."

"Hey! What's going on over there?" A young man had just come out of the YMCA.

"Crap," Wally muttered under his breath, then shouted, "These men are hurt!" Somehow he made his voice sound younger than it normally did, and it normally sounded pretty young. "Call 911! I think they were fighting!"

"Got it!" the young man shouted back. "Cindy at the desk knows first-aid – I'll send her out!"

He went back inside. "Run," Wally said. He grabbed Ariane's hand.

She staggered after him. They hurried across railroad tracks and the street behind them, and into the trees on the other side. At first her legs felt like rubber, but the surge of adrenaline she felt as a black-and-white police car with "O.P.P." on its door screamed past, siren wailing, red and blue lights flashing, galvanized them.

"Hold up," she gasped once they were hidden among the trees. "I think I can get us out of here now."

Wally nodded. He leaned over, hands on his knees. "I can't believe I just beat up Emeka," he said between gasps for air. "And the other guy. How'd I do that?"

"Emeka?"

"The big black guy. Met him when I was living with Rex Major." Wally's voice shook. "That's the second one of Major's men I've clobbered over the head. I didn't even think about what to do, I just...did it. How?"

"It's the sword," Ariane said. "You're an heir of Arthur." She heard the tremor in her own voice. "Excalibur just saved us...saved me."

"Why are you so late?" Wally said then, almost angrily. "I ate KFC and drank a Coke and made them both last as long as possible and I was still getting the evil eye from the girls at the counter. You should have been here two hours ago!"

"Blizzard," Ariane said. "We were slow getting to Medicine Hat." She took a deep breath. "Which is where we should be getting back to."

"We're fully dressed," Wally pointed out. "We can't pop up in the Medicine Hat Lodge pool like this. Not with all those windows looking down on us."

Ariane nodded. "I know," she said. She looked up into the swirling snow. "So change fast."

Wally groaned. "You're not kidding, are you?"

"Nope." She gave him a big smile. "Will you go first, or shall I?"

"I will," Wally said. "Turn your back."

She did so, staring across the road. There were trees between her and the Y, but some flashing red light made its way through the screen. She wondered what Emeka and the other man would say to the authorities, once they were able to talk. *Nothing that involves Rex Major, I'll bet. They wouldn't dare mention his name.*

"Done," Wally said. His voice shook again, but this time it sounded as though his teeth were chattering. "Hurry up."

Ariane turned around. He stood in his swim trunks, body pale and white in the dim light, arms wrapped around his scrawny chest. She unbuttoned and unzipped her jeans, and Wally's eyes widened. He turned away in a hurry. Ariane laughed. "Don't worry," she said. "I'm wearing my swimsuit under my clothes."

"Oh," he said. But he still didn't turn back as she pulled off her clothes. She found that endearing. *So chivalrous...of course,* he *is a descendant of King Arthur. Or at least we think so.*

She stuffed her clothes and shoes into her backpack. "It is c-cold, isn't it-t?" she said, teeth already chattering, as Wally turned around to face her again.

"I-is it-t?" he chattered back. "I ha-hadn't no-noticed."

She reached out and took his hand. "Then let's g-get out of h-here."

Holding tight to him, she let the wet ground suck them down and away.

◆◆ ◆▶

A sound like thunder grumbled just at the edge of Rex Major's awareness, explosions or a car chase or overwrought music from some superhero extravaganza playing in the media room. For all they didn't get along, Felicia Knight and her brother, Wally, seemed to share the same execrable taste in movies.

Major found it irritating – he'd lived alone a long time,

and having someone sharing his condo, even though it was a very, very large condo, grated on him – but the irritation was minor. Especially in light of the information he'd just received from Gerald MacKenzie, Emeka's companion on the long-shot mission to Gravenhurst he'd thought had some minor possibility of netting Wally Knight.

It sounded like the two men had come very close to grabbing, not just the boy, but the girl as well...but not close enough. Emeka lay in hospital, with a concussion and four stitches in his scalp. MacKenzie had apparently suffered a "minor injury," the details of which he hadn't seen fit to share with Rex Major. What interested Major about all of that, though, was that the injuries had been inflicted solely by Wally Knight: Ariane's powers had had nothing to do with them, because she'd been taken out of the picture by Emeka's chloroform-soaked cloth the moment she'd appeared. Major had told Emeka to be prepared for the possibility she would show up, and it sounded as if his idea of how to capture her had almost worked. Clearly, if they took her by surprise and knocked her out before she could act, they could then spirit her away and imprison her somewhere where her powers would do her no good.

Rather like that damned tree Viviane locked me up in for what should have been the best centuries of my life, Major thought sourly.

Wally Knight, true to his surname, had raced to the aid of his damsel in distress, and succeeded in rescuing her from two grown, trained fighting men. *Arthur's blood runs in his veins, for sure and certain,* Major thought. He glanced up from the terminal at the open door from his office into the living room. Although he couldn't see it from there, the media room was just beyond. And he knew Arthur's blood ran in Flish's veins, as well. He had proved that when, with both of them holding the second shard of Excalibur, he had had the power to heal the girl's broken leg. Broken by Ariane.

Felicia Knight had moved out on her own as soon as her parents had separated. That being the case, Rex Major had been under no compulsion to inform her parents of her whereabouts, but he had done so, all the same. Of course, he had infused that conversation with the Voice of Command that was one of his principal remaining magical powers, one that had grown stronger as more and more of the shards of Excalibur were found. Even if he couldn't draw directly on the power of the shard he had in his possession while Ariane held the other two they had thus far found.

Felicia's parents – he never called her "Flish" as Wally did, knowing how she hated that nickname – were very pleased that he had "taken her under his wing" and had offered her employment in his offices (not that he had done any such thing), and hoped that with his "guidance and support" she would soon be enrolling in the University of Toronto and studying...something or other. Slightly befuddled by the magic he had used to calm them, they were a bit unclear as to what kind of career she might pursue.

He *did* have a career in mind for her, though he wasn't about to share the knowledge with her parents. *Warleader of the Armies of Faerie Liberation* had a nice ring to it, he thought. He frowned. Or maybe not. WAFL would be bound to be pronounced "waffle," and what kind of terror would a name like that invoke?

Well, he'd have his PR people work on it.

Wally and Flish's parents, meanwhile, were equally convinced, along with the Canadian media, that their wayward son had vanished in New Zealand. Wally's face had been spread across the country via newspapers, the Web, and television...though never with any mention of Rex Major, of course. Which meant there was always the chance someone would recognize Wally, wherever he popped up. Since he was supposed to be dead in the southern hemisphere, the chance was probably small, but still, it might crimp Wally's and Ariane's activities a *little* bit – and crimping their activities was exactly what Major was trying to do.

He sighed. He still didn't have a clue where the fourth shard might be hidden. Neither, he was certain, did Ariane. She might have the power of the Lady of the Lake, but he had one shard of his own, and it too would call out to the not-yet-discovered fourth shard. He could not use it to find the two Ariane held – the Lady's power would not permit that – but he should be able to use it to find the fourth.

Of course, so should she.

But the fourth had not surfaced, and that made him uneasy. Though the Lady had to have hidden the shards originally in some place accessible through fresh water, that had been a millennium ago. The fourth shard could be at the bottom of the ocean, where the salt water all around it would preclude either him *or* Ariane from finding it – at least while neither of them had a complete set of the shards found thus far.

With all three shards in his possession, he thought even the ocean would not be sufficient to keep the fourth hidden – but he had only one, and Ariane had two.

He could not take the shards from her by force. She had to give them willingly. Nor could he kill her; to do so would drain all power from the shards, rendering them nothing but inert pieces of corroded metal.

But what he *could* do was find another hostage. Ariane's weakness, as he had proved over and over, was her concern for other people. She had given him a shard when he had threatened Wally, though she had later stolen it back. She had given the second shard to Wally himself – who had soon been gulled into handing it over to Major – but the false camaraderie he had fostered with the boy that had made that possible had collapsed. Wally had not managed to steal the second shard away from him. But the boy *had* managed to help Ariane claim the third shard, although for a while, with Aunt Phyllis as his hostage, Merlin had thought he had that one in the bag.

He needed both of the shards she held in order to find the fourth. That meant he needed another hostage.

Which had led him to send Emeka and Mackenzie to Gravenhurst, when the skein of magic he had woven through the Internet via his Excalibur Computer Systems server software had flagged a series of searches for towns with both swimming pools and libraries, culminating in considerable research into the Gravenhurst YMCA. It had been a shot in the dark, but the town was only a couple of hours away, so why not?

And he had almost hit the jackpot. Except Wally had proven more capable than he had expected.

But Merlin had still learned something valuable. *Anesthetize Ariane, and she cannot function. Knock her out, and move her to a dry room, and she will be helpless. And though I cannot kill her directly, I can starve her until she gives in.*

If I can get both of them at once, even better: then I will have a hostage to use against her. If I can get only her, Wally will certainly try to stage a rescue – and when he fails, then, once again, I'll have a hostage.

He leaned back in his chair and steepled his fingers. *I may have missed her this time. But next time she appears, I will be ready for her. We will be ready for her.*

Perhaps a Taser instead of chloroform...

His email program dinged, notifying him of a new message. His eyes strayed lazily to the corner of the screen where a preview had just popped up. What he saw there made him straighten in a hurry.

The subject line was innocuous: ECS Automated System

Report. But only one system message used that subject, and it had nothing to do with servers or routers or DNS or any of the other arcane building blocks of the world-wide computer network, which Major didn't really understand but had profited greatly from nonetheless.

ECS Automated System Report was the subject line generated when *his* magic, borne by the Internet, came into contact with a much more powerful magic: the magic of Excalibur.

He'd received a message with just that subject line when Wally Knight had carried his smartphone close to the Lady of the Lake on the day she manifested herself to Wally and Ariane in Regina's Wascana Lake. He'd received a second from the Northwest Territories, when some piece of Internet-connected equipment had been brought close enough to the hidden first shard of Excalibur. He'd received a third from the south of France, when scientists studying paintings in an ancient cave complex had come close to the second shard. The third shard he'd found by forcing Ariane to locate it. But now here was the same subject line, and that meant...

The fourth shard.

As usual, the only text in the message was an IP address, the address of the device whose tiny sliver of Merlin's magic had been triggered by its proximity to the fourth shard. Major turned to his computer.

The IP address belonged to Cacibajagua Island Diving Adventures. A few more clicks of the mouse, and he was looking at the company's website. "Dive with us!" it read. "Diving adventures for everyone from the beginning snorkeller to the certified cave diver. Dive lessons from beginner to advanced. Don't want to dive? Enjoy a scenic cave tour in our state-of-the-art submarine!"

Hmm, Major thought. He clicked the "About Us" link.

"Cacibajagua is a Taino word which, in Taino mythology,

refers to the cave where life began," he read. "Our company was founded by the world-renowned cave diver Audron Rounsavall, who discovered on this tiny island one of the world's most beautiful underwater caves, a unique cavern below sea level and filled with seawater, but also accessible from inland, where fresh water flows into it, tumbling down as a spectacular cascade through the cave ceiling into a beautiful saltwater pool. Audron was so taken with the cave and with the island that he bought it and started Cacibajagua Island Diving Adventures, so people from all over the world can enjoy the cave and the other outstanding diving opportunities on this and nearby islands and reefs. Call us today and arrange for your unforgettable island diving adventure!"

Major's heart speeded. *The fourth shard*, he thought. *It's in that cave. I'd bet my magic on it.*

And it was surrounded by salt water. Which meant Ariane Forsythe didn't know where it was – *couldn't* know, unless someone brought it to the surface. This time, he'd have it first, and keep it. This time, Ariane and Wally couldn't interfere.

With two shards in his possession, and with Felicia, as much heir to Arthur as Wally, to help him draw on their power, he would find the final piece of the sword, the hilt, and claim it for his own. He rubbed the ruby stud in his earlobe. *Today, Excalibur. Tomorrow, the world,* he thought. He chuckled at his own pretentiousness, but added anyway, out loud, "And then...Faerie."

He got up and headed to the media room to let Felicia know she was about to get an unexpected Caribbean vacation. As he crossed the living room, the soundtrack of the movie she was watching swelled to a thunderous, triumphant climax.

The noise no longer bothered him. In fact, it suited his mood perfectly.

CHAPTER FOUR

A KISS ON THE CHEEK

ARIANE WAITED IN THE NEBULOUS NOTHINGNESS of the strange watery realm into which she dissolved when she travelled using the Lady's power. She knew Wally was with her; she always interpreted the sensation as him holding her hand, as he had been when they'd left Gravenhurst, but of course they didn't really have hands in any material sense at the moment. As far as she knew.

One thing that always felt just as solid and sharp as ever was the shard of Excalibur she carried. Since she had two to Major's one, she could draw on the power of this one. Through it, she could also sense the second shard in her possession, though it was currently tucked away under the mattress of her bed at Barringer Farm. She couldn't call on the power of both shards, not unless Wally was holding them. Somehow, his connection to King Arthur also gave him a connection to the sword, through which it transmitted even more of its power.

She didn't need any of the shard's power for this little jaunt halfway across the country using waterways and water systems. But that sharp, constant presence protected her in another way. Whenever she used the Lady's power, she felt the water's distant and insistent call: to let herself dissolve, to release the spark that made her an individual and join the mindless flow of water around the world. She had to guard against that dangerous, insidious urge every time. The shard helped. It had no intention of letting itself vanish into liquid darkness. Its steely determination – *literally* steely – helped her hang on to herself – and to Wally.

Now, with the finer control of her powers that had been developing over the past few weeks, she held the two of them in limbo, waiting for the pool below the water-slides at the Medicine Hat Lodge to clear. The moment it did so, she brought them into it, the surge from their arrival masked by the ordinary rush and roil of water.

They made their way to the side of the pool, tossed out their backpacks – Ariane ordering them dry in the same instant – and then climbed, still sopping wet, out onto the brown tiles of the poolside, just as a small boy came squealing off the end of one of the slides and splashed into the water behind them.

They hurried away from the pool. In one of the many plastic chairs around the edges of the big open room, close to the almost-empty leisure pool and beneath an entirely superfluous beach umbrella, sat Emma, reading a book, two fluffy white towels on the table beside her. She looked up at them, marking her place with her finger, as they plodded wetly over to her and grabbed a towel apiece.

"You took longer than I expected," she said quietly. "I was beginning to worry."

"Rex Major," Ariane said. She rubbed her hair vigorously. She would have preferred to just wish herself dry – she never used a towel any more when she showered – but for the sake of appearances she supposed she could put up with this more primitive method for the moment. "He twigged to the fact Wally was there. We barely got away." She didn't mention the chloroform or the fact Wally had clobbered Emeka with a tree branch.

Emma looked alarmed. "Does he know where you're hiding out?"

"I don't see how he can," Wally said. "Even our pool search was done a long way from the farm." He sounded tired and a little shaky, and Ariane, looking at him in the light, suddenly realized how pale his face looked. Every freckle on it – and there were quite a lot, even though the summer's sun was now barely a memory – stood out like a brown dot on white paper.

"Is it still storming?" Ariane said. She looked up at the windows that surrounded the pool courtyard just below the high ceiling, but could see only darkness.

"It is," Emma said. "Worse than ever. We're stuck here overnight." She gave Wally a long hard look. "You look terrible. What exactly happened?"

"Later," Ariane said hastily. "Wally needs something to eat. So do I. And sleep."

"I'm all right," Wally said, but he didn't look all right. And then he blinked. "I almost forgot," he breathed. "With everything else that happened... Ariane, I've got a lead."

"A lead?" For a minute Ariane didn't understand what he was talking about, then she gasped. *"Mom?"*

Wally nodded. "Just before Emeka showed up in the library. I found a couple of photos. A face, out of focus, in the background, but the software thinks it's her, and so do I."

"Out of focus, in the background, *where?*" Ariane's heart pounded, raced in a way it hadn't even when she was running from Rex Major's men. "Wally, where?"

"Horseshoe Bay, B.C.," Wally said. "Where the ferries leave for Vancouver Island. She was there two weeks ago, anyway."

"We have to go find her!" Ariane looked back at the

pool, already thinking about plunging back into it, heading west, finding Mom...

Mom, who had shown up wet and disoriented on the doorstep after her walk around the lake two years ago, and ended up in the psych ward at the Regina General Hospital. Mom, who had pretended not to know her daughter when Ariane had gone to visit her. Mom, who had somehow escaped the hospital and disappeared, leaving Ariane to the care of a series of foster parents until Aunt Phyllis had recovered from her cancer treatments enough to look after her...

Someone grabbed her arm. She felt a surge of anger at the touch and the water in the leisure pool swirled and gurgled, eliciting sharp cries from the small children there. "Ariane!"

It was Emma. Ariane came back to herself and forced her anger down. The sword was fuelling it; her mother had rejected the quest to reforge Excalibur, and the sword knew it – and resented it.

I control the sword, Ariane told herself. *It doesn't control me.* The water subsided. Confused chatter erupted from the parents. Ariane ignored it, staring into Emma's warm brown eyes.

"You can't go off half-cocked," Emma said softly. "You have to plan." She glanced at Wally. "And look at Wally. He can't go anywhere tonight anyway. We'll eat, we'll talk, we'll decide what to do, we'll sleep on it."

"But you *will* let us go," Ariane said. She supposed it should have been a question, but it came out as a flat statement. No one was going to stop her from going to look for her mother. *No one.*

"Of course I will," Emma said. Then she smiled a little. "As if I could stop you." She closed her book with a snap and stood up. "Let's go to our rooms. You need to get dressed. Then food."

Ariane slung her backpack over her shoulder, Wally took his, and together they followed Emma out of the pool room. It wasn't a long walk: Emma had gotten them two rooms on the main floor – apparently the Lodge wasn't very full at the moment. Emma gave Wally his key, and he went into his room while Ariane went into hers and Emma's to change back into her clothes. Once Wally emerged from his room, dressed in his normal geek-culture clothes and not quite as pale as he had been, they all went down the hall to the lobby and then into the hotel's buffet restaurant. Ariane felt ravenous, as she usually did after using her powers, and filled her plate to overflowing, although she found the brown/ochre/orange colour scheme of the dining room unappetizing. Another side effect of the Lady's powers, she suspected. Red used to be her favorite colour. Now she gravitated toward blues and greens.

Wally, though usually just as big an eater as the stereotypical growing teenage boy was supposed to be – and he *was* growing; at least five centimetres since the adventure had begun – took very little, almost as little as Emma, who ate like the proverbial bird.

They didn't talk much while they ate. With several other people in the restaurant, discretion was in order. They returned to Wally's room once they were done. Since it had only a single bed, there was space in it for a big armchair, a sofa and a coffee table, whereas Emma's and Ariane's room had only a couple of chairs nestled up to a small round table by the window.

Emma and Wally sat on the couch, while Ariane plopped into the chair. "I phoned Phyllis and told her we'd be spending the night, and that Wally made it back safely," Emma said. "I didn't tell her about Rex Major's men almost nabbing you in Gravenhurst. No reason to worry her when she's all alone except for the dog and cats."

"Did you tell her Wally spotted Mom?" Ariane said. Emma shook her head. "No. And I won't until I know more." She looked at Wally. "So tell me more. What did you find, and how did you find it?"

◄◄ ►►

Wally had never felt more tired in his life. Tired, and strangely shaken. He'd taken down both of Rex Major's trained bodyguards with nothing more than a stick. He hadn't even thought about what he was doing. He hadn't *had* to think about it. The moves had come naturally to him, as though he had practised them all his life.

Sure, he'd taken a high-school fencing course, but he'd never been all that good at it – not until the first shard of Excalibur had been found. Then suddenly Natasha Mueller, his fencing coach, had been all prepared to send him off to the Chinook Open tournament in Swift Current. Instead, he'd fallen on some ice and knocked himself out, so that had been the end of that. Plus then there had come the trip to France and his betrayal of Ariane, then the move to Toronto with Rex Major, followed by his escape from Rex Major and the rescue of Aunt Phyllis in Prince Albert and the recovery of the second shard in New Zealand and the flight to Cypress Hills, and now the series of trips to libraries in towns with swimming pools.

Suffice it to say, he hadn't exactly been practising.

Yet he had no doubt that if he were given a sword right now, he could compete with the best fencers in the world. He frowned. Except, of course, he'd be disqualified. You couldn't duck under someone's guard and clobber them from behind in competitive fencing, as he had done with Emeka. Or, for that matter, hit them below the belt as he had the first guy. In retrospect, he cringed a little in sympathy. But he'd felt no sympathy when he'd attacked: nothing but righteous anger and determination to rescue Ariane.

The damsel in distress, he thought, looking at her now. Although, with the powers of the Lady of the Lake at her command, she was about as far from a shrinking-violet, days-of-yore maiden as you could get.

That hadn't changed how he'd felt, though, when he'd gone at Rex Major's two henchmen.

He remembered the solid thud when his branch had hit the back of Emeka's head, the way the impact had shivered up the wood into his hands. He could still feel it. He remembered the blood. It was like the business with the security guard outside Rex Major's condo all over again. That guy he'd hit with a poker. He'd thought he might have killed him. Rex Major had assured him he hadn't. He hoped he hadn't killed Emeka. He didn't want to kill anyone. But with the sword now singing in his blood as well as in Ariane's, though in a different way, he was afraid sometime he would act without thinking, and...

He realized Emma and Ariane were looking at him expectantly. He blinked at Ariane. "What?" he said.

"Tell us how you found the pictures of Mom," Ariane said impatiently. "Honestly, Wally, what's wrong with you?"

Wally felt a flash of uncharacteristic anger toward her and almost snapped something he'd almost certainly have regretted – but bit it off just in time. That, too, felt like the sword talking.

Rex Major had been able to convince him to give up the second shard of the sword, retrieved from a cave complex in southern France, because Ariane had badly hurt Flish and because Wally had been afraid Ariane wouldn't be able to control what the sword wanted her to do – to *become*. Now he knew exactly how she'd felt. "A thing of war," the Lady had called it, and there was no doubt that was exactly what it was, and how it wanted to be used.

"I'm just...tired," he said. He'd talk to Ariane about what he was feeling in more detail sometime later, when they were alone. Emma didn't want Aunt Phyllis to worry, but Wally didn't want *Emma* to worry. The grown-ups couldn't do anything to help. They had no part in this war – and he guessed that war was what they were waging – but to provide logistical support. If they exposed their location, they'd simply become hostages.

"Okay," he said, gathering his thoughts. "So I used that photo you gave me and plugged it into this new image search engine I found..."

When he had finished explaining, Ariane got up. "Let's go," she said. "Let's go right now. Rex Major could already be –"

"You'll do no such thing," Emma said. "Rex Major probably doesn't know where she is."

"If I can find her using the Web, he can," Wally said.

"Maybe. But you haven't really found her, have you? You've found where she was two weeks ago. You don't know where she lives, what name she's using, anything that will really help you find her. Ferries leave Horseshoe Bay every day, and for more places than just Nanaimo. It's also close to Vancouver. She could be anywhere in the world by now. You need to plan what you're going to do when you get there, how you're going to try to find her if she's there, or find out where she went if she isn't." Her voice softened. "Besides, Wally is exhausted. Look at him. You need to replenish your energy, too. And what could you possibly do to find her in Horseshoe Bay in the middle of the night?"

"But we know where she is," Ariane cried. "How can I just sit here knowing that? How can I sleep?"

"You know where she *was*," Emma said.

"I think there's a pretty good chance she's still there,"

Wally said. "Since she was there long enough to show up in two different pictures a few days apart."

"Then she'll still be there tomorrow."

"But if Rex Major *does* know where she is, every second may count," Ariane protested.

"He can't find her in the dark either," Emma said.

"And at least we know he doesn't have her yet," Wally put in.

"How?" Ariane demanded.

"Because if he had her, he wouldn't have tried to grab us both in Gravenhurst," Wally said. "He would have just given us a message: give me the two shards you have or..." He didn't finish the sentence.

Ariane pressed her lips into a stubborn frown. "Still..."

"Sleep," Emma said. "Rest. Go in the morning. See what you can find."

Wally was suddenly seized by a huge, jaw-cracking yawn. When he could talk again, he said, "Please, Ariane."

Ariane's expression softened. "All right," she said, albeit still reluctantly. "Tomorrow."

"Still nothing on the fourth-shard front?" Wally said.

Ariane shook her head. "No," she said. "Wherever it is, I can't sense it."

Wally chewed on his lower lip. "I wish I could say that means Major can't have a lead on it either, but I can't. All it would take is someone with an Internet-connected smartphone to get too close to it, and he'll feel the tug like a spider feels its web vibrate when an insect lands on it."

"No way for us to know," Ariane said. "Either I hear the shard singing to me and we go get it before Major does, or Major finds it...and then I hear it and we steal it back from him. We can't worry about that right now. We have to worry about Mom."

Wally nodded, but he hardly heard her. He'd suddenly

had an idea. He wasn't sure it was a good idea. In fact, he thought it might be a spectacularly bad idea. Which was why he wasn't going to tell Ariane about it. He wasn't even sure he was going to act on it.

That's a lie, he told himself then. *You know darn well you're going to act on it.* "I really need to get to bed," he said out loud. He yawned again, though more for effect than because he needed to; the surge of adrenaline accompanying his idea had momentarily rejuvenated him. "What time do you want to get up?"

"We're two hours ahead of the West Coast right now," Emma said.

"And you're right, there's no point in getting there in the dark," Ariane said reluctantly. "Let's head out around ten."

"I can almost sleep in, then," Wally said. "Best news I've heard all day."

"Good night, Wally," Emma said. She looked at Ariane. "Coming?"

"In a minute."

"All right." Emma went out.

Ariane looked at Wally. "Thank you," she said softly. "For tonight. When Emeka grabbed me, put that cloth over me...If you hadn't been there..."

"Your knight in shining armour," Wally said. He felt both warmed and strangely embarrassed by her praise.

She leaned close. He suddenly knew how a deer in the headlights felt. She kissed his cheek, her lips warm and soft against his skin. She leaned back again. "Good night." She got up and went to the door. "See you in the morning," she said, and went out.

Wally wanted to say good night, but his throat wouldn't work.

Well, he thought. *Well.*

Well.

He shook his head violently. *It was just a kiss on the cheek*, he thought. *It wasn't a kiss kiss. Even Flish used to kiss me on the cheek...back when she still liked me.*

But he could feel the touch of Ariane's lips lingering against his skin.

He took a deep breath. He still thought the idea that had come to him while he was talking to Ariane and Emma might be a really, really bad one. But he was going to try it, anyway.

He went to the room phone, lifted it, and dialed nine. When he heard the dial tone, he punched in *67 – so that the hotel's number wouldn't show up on Caller ID on the phone on the other end, which he had good reason to think Rex Major would be monitoring – and then a number he hadn't called in weeks.

One ring. Two. And then...

"Hello?" said a man's voice on the other end.

Wally hesitated another moment. Then he said, "Hello, Dad."

◄► ►

Ariane licked her lips as she walked to her room next door. She hadn't even known she was going to do that until she'd done it. But it had felt right.

Actually, it had felt great.

It was just a peck on the cheek, she thought. *A thank-you kiss. Nothing else.*

And that was true, but it had felt like more than that to her. And she suspected it had felt like more than that to Wally, too.

She let herself into the room. Emma was in the bathroom. Ariane walked to the window and looked out into the pool area. She could feel the tug of the water, could sense everybody still swimming in it. Even from there, she could have reached out and pulled that water to her, drawn it into tentacles, used it to defend herself from any of Rex Major's men who might make an appearance.

Not that that was likely. Major had no way of knowing they were in Medicine Hat.

Did he?

She sighed. Paranoia ran deep when your adversary was rich, powerful *and* a legendary sorcerer. She wouldn't have thought he could have figured out Wally was in Gravenhurst – but he had.

She closed the curtain and turned back to face the hotel room, but she wasn't really seeing it. Instead, she felt the bright power of the shard of Excalibur strapped to her side, and heard the more distant song of the second shard, tucked away at Barringer Farm. She couldn't sense the one Major had, but just the thought of it in his possession angered her. It wasn't *right*, Major having one of the shards. It wasn't what the sword wanted. It wasn't what the Lady had wanted, the Lady who had forged the sword to begin with.

And it definitely wasn't what Ariane wanted, now that *she* was the Lady.

Yet for all her power, she could not simply attack Major and take the shard from him. He had power, too, more than he had had when this all began. Simply having three of the shards of Excalibur once more at play in the world had allowed more magic to seep through the opening between Faerie and Earth. Major had healed Flish's broken leg. His power of Command could weave complex illusions around ordinary people, like Aunt Phyllis and, presumably, Wally's parents, or anyone else he needed to influence. And, of course, he was also one of the richest men in the world, with all the security arrangements and resources that came with that. Attacking him directly would surely be disastrous, and that was without even considering the fact he had Flish at his side, and Flish, however much she hated Ariane, however estranged she might be from Wally, was still Wally's sister.

Not only that, Flish was, like Wally, an heir of Arthur's. And if Wally had developed surprising fighting skills due to the power of the sword, who knew what his sister was now capable of?

No, Ariane's and Wally's path remained the same. They needed the fourth shard. With three in her possession, Ariane was confident nothing would keep her from finding the final piece, the hilt, and with every piece of the sword but one in her possession, she would be able to simply draw the final shard to her, no matter what effort Merlin expended to keep it from her.

But the fourth shard remained invisible to her. It could be anywhere: Antarctica, the Himalayas, Zaire, the Amazon. The world was a very big place, and the Lady, Ariane knew – for she had proven it herself – could have travelled anywhere around it.

At least we've got a lead on Mom, she thought fiercely. *Who cares about Excalibur if I can just find her?*

Wearing her long flannel nightgown, Emma came out of the washroom. Ariane started toward it to change into her pajamas, but she didn't get far; there came a knock on the door, frantic, urgent.

She went to it, looked through the peephole, and saw Wally, wide-eyed and wild-looking, on the other side. She opened it, and he burst in.

"I think Rex Major knows where the fourth shard is!" he said. "And I do, too!"

CHAPTER FIVE

WALLY PHONES HOME

"WALLY?" WALLY COULDN'T SEE his father, but he knew him well enough to know his eyes had just jerked wide. "*Wally?*"

"Yeah," Wally said.

"Thank God you're alive! What's going on? Where are you?"

"I'm safe," Wally said. "I'm okay."

"That's not good enough," his father said, and now Wally could imagine his eyes narrowing, his thick black brows drawing together. "Your mother and I have been worried sick. You ran away from Rex Major's condo in Toronto. You flew to New Zealand, for God's sake! Dozens of people searched the mountains for you. No one could find a trace of you. They told us you were probably dead –"

"I had good reason to run away from Rex Major."

His father snorted. "Don't you *dare* try to blame this on Mr. Major. He's an amazing man. He's been nothing but kind to this family. He's looking after your sister right now, helping her get a start in his company."

Voice of Command, Wally reminded himself, pushing

back against swelling anger. *Dad's under Major's thumb. He'd never be that trusting, that brainwashed, if he wasn't...well, brainwashed.* "It wasn't his fault," he said out loud, as evenly as he could. "I just...had a chance to do something special. I took it."

"You're not making sense," Dad said.

"I'm sorry," Wally said, and he was. He hated lying to his father. But with Dad under Command, anything he said might make it back to Major. "I really am. Is Mom okay?"

A moment's hesitation. "As far as I know," Dad said. "I haven't actually spoken to her for...a couple of weeks."

Torture couldn't have made Wally ask Dad how Erica, the blonde his father had left Mom for, was doing, even though he supposed she was somewhere nearby. "Tell her I'm all right."

"I will," Dad said. "But Wally, we have to know where you are. You aren't old enough to –"

"I can look after myself," Wally said. "That's all you need to know." He paused. *Here we go*, he thought. *The real reason I called.* "How's Flish? Is she still in Toronto?"

The idea that had come to him moments before had been simple: possibly stupid, but simple. Major would take Flish with him if he knew where the fourth shard was and wanted to retrieve it. He had to have her with him if he was going to use the power of the shard he already had, and he'd want her with him if he found the fourth shard so he could use its power, too. Without ready access to the Internet, it was much harder to keep tabs on Major's whereabouts than it might have been otherwise. But if Major were intent on keeping his parents calm and in his corner, he just might have told them wherever he might be taking Flish. *If. Might.*

"Flish is doing wonderfully," Dad said, so enthusiastically Wally knew it was in response to the Command Merlin had placed on him. "You won't believe where Major is taking her."

Wally's hand tensed on the phone. "Where?" he said, as calmly as he could, though it felt as if an alarm clock were jangling inside his head.

"The Caribbean," Dad said. "Mr. Major called to tell me she's been doing so wonderfully in her new job that he wants to reward her with a trip. They're leaving Sunday morning."

The Caribbean? That was an awfully big area. "Did she say where in the Caribbean?"

"No," Dad said. "Why?"

"Just curious." Wally paused. "And...you're all right with this? Your eighteen-year-old daughter flying off with an older man to the Caribbean?" *And you have no idea just how* much *older.*

"Stop it, Wally," Dad snapped. "Mr. Major is a perfect gentleman, as you well know. I don't appreciate your insinuations."

"Dad –"

"I'm glad you're all right. But you have to tell us where you are. The police have you listed as a missing person...presumed dead. Just turn yourself in to the authorities wherever you are and –"

"Dad, I'm all right. Honestly. You can tell them you heard from me."

"You're underage, Wally. Turn yourself in. Or just come home."

"There's nobody in our home, Dad," Wally said, the anger swelling up in him again. "You left it and Mom is who-knows-where –"

"Los Angeles," Dad said. "New movie."

"Los Angeles," Wally said. "Why would I go home?"

"I mean come to where I am," Dad said.

"And where's that?"

"I'm in Victoria. At the Fairmont Empress."

Victoria. Wally almost laughed. *And we're heading to Horseshoe Bay. I could hop a ferry.*

"I can't, Dad," he said. "Not yet."

An intake of breath. "Wally..."

"No, Dad."

A pause. "I'll tell the police you're alive. They're going to start looking again. They'll find you eventually."

"Maybe," Wally said. "But you'd be surprised how much I move around."

Another pause.

"Goodbye, Dad," he said finally, when his Dad didn't speak. There didn't seem to be anything else left to say. "I'll call again."

"Wally –"

Wally hung up.

He took a deep breath. The anger boiled up inside, choking him. Some of it was aimed at his father, who had left his mother for a younger woman. Some of it was aimed at his mother, who had always put her career ahead of her family. But most of it was aimed at Major, who was meddling with his family, making what was already pretty dysfunctional even worse.

Then he remembered what he'd just learned, and he jumped to his feet.

Rex Major was taking Flish to the Caribbean, and he could think of only one possible reason: Rex Major knew where the fourth shard of Excalibur was.

He ran for the door.

◄◄ ►►

Ariane and Emma listened as Wally explained, Ariane with growing excitement, dread – and frustration. *"Damn his Internet magic. I still can't sense the thing and he* knows where it is!"

"Language, Ariane," Emma said, sounding for a moment exactly like the strict schoolteacher she used to be. "So does this mean a change of plans for you two?"

Ariane looked at her. She sat there, tall and rather gaunt, her short white hair a little ruffled now since she'd pulled on her nightgown. Ariane didn't know how old she was. She seemed unflappable.

But she was vulnerable, just like Aunt Phyllis, to Rex Major and his voice of Command. So far as they knew, Major had no idea Emma existed. Ariane vowed silently to keep it that way. *The last thing we need is to hand Major another potential hostage.*

"I don't know," Ariane said miserably. "What about Mom?"

"Major doesn't have her yet, or he'd find a way to let us know," Wally said. "He has my email address, and he knows I'm checking in on computers regularly. There's been nothing. Not even threats."

"I guess..." Ariane said. *Mom...* She longed to chase the lead Wally had discovered, however uncertain it might be. But the best way to keep her mom, and Aunt Phyllis, and Emma from becoming hostages again was to defeat Major completely, and claim the sword for herself. If he had two shards and she had two, it would all come down to the hilt. But if she had three shards, she could surely find the hilt almost immediately, and with it in her possession, could supposedly call the remaining shard to her – whatever that meant.

"The Caribbean is a big place," she said after a minute. "How do we figure out where he's going?"

"Same way I found out he was going to New Zealand," Wally said. "He'll take his private jet. He has to register a flight plan...and flight plans are searchable. We'll know where he's going before he's even left, at least in general terms. We just have to be waiting for him, and then follow him."

"And Flish."

"And Flish," Wally said.

"If he finds out you're close behind him, he might use *her* as a hostage," Emma warned.

"Then we won't let him find out we're there until it's too late," Wally said. "We won't let anything happen to her." He looked at Ariane. "Right?"

Ariane knew the unspoken reason behind his questioning look. She'd hurt Flish badly in Regina when Flish and the coven of mean girls she'd hung out with had tried to attack Ariane on the tennis courts near Oscana Collegiate. It had driven a rift between her and Wally that had led directly to his deciding to throw in, for a time, with Rex Major – which was why Major had the one shard he held.

Flish would have no qualms about hurting me, Ariane thought. *And maybe Wally, too – even though he doesn't want to believe it – if Merlin has his hooks deep enough into her. After all, Wally hurt* me *when he was on Merlin's side, stealing the shard from me, convinced it was for my own good. Merlin's Voice of Command may not work on the younger Knights, but he can be plenty persuasive even without magic.*

But she didn't say that out loud. *I control the sword; it doesn't control me*, she told herself for the umpteenth time, and tried to think it as though she meant it, even as her memory conjured up the way the water of the pools in Gravenhurst and this hotel had bubbled and swirled when she got upset. *Even if Flish attacks me, I won't hurt her. Much.*

"Right," she said.

Wally took a deep breath. "Then we'll need computer access tomorrow," he said.

Emma frowned. "There's probably a business centre

somewhere in the hotel, although I've never –"

"Not here," Ariane said. She'd suddenly had a wild notion, a way to maybe have her cake and eat it, too. "Too dangerous. Too close to Barringer Farm."

"Then where?" Wally said.

Ariane met his gaze squarely. "How about West Vancouver?"

"West...?" Wally blinked. "Ohhh...you mean Horseshoe Bay."

"We need a computer a long way from here. We can kill two birds with one stone. It can't hurt to take a quick look around. Maybe we'll get lucky." *Mom...*

"What if Rex Major figures out you're out there?" Emma said quietly. "Won't that be dangerous, too? For you *and* her?"

"He'll just know we're using a computer again. He won't know we're there because we think Mom might be there," Ariane said.

Emma and Wally looked at each other, then at Ariane, together. "You're the boss," Wally said. He grinned crookedly. "My Lady."

"Don't call me that," Ariane said, surprising herself with the heat in her voice. Wally looked startled.

"I'm sorry, it was just a –"

"I'm *not* the Lady of the Lake. I have her power. For now. But the sooner we can get rid of it, the better. The sooner we can get all of this magic out of our world, the better. The sooner I can go back to just being an ordinary girl, the better."

Wally raised his hands. "All right, all right. I said I was sorry."

Ariane took a deep breath, trying to release her anger. In the bathroom, the toilet gurgled.

The sound frightened her. *I control the sword; it doesn't control me*, she thought again. But was that true?

And for all her brave words, did she *really* want to give up the power of the Lady of the Lake? The power to make water do her bidding, the power to travel anywhere in the world she wanted? Did she really want to go back to being Ariane Forsythe, the "foster brat" who was teased at every school she went to?

I'm not a foster brat anymore, she thought. *I've got Aunt Phyllis. And soon I'll have Mom. And I'll give up all this magic in a minute if it means I can live with her like we used to, go back to being a normal family.*

"I'm sorry, too," she said. She longed to leap up and let the water take them to Horseshoe Bay right then, but there was still no point in getting there in the dark. And they both needed rest. Rex Major wasn't flying to the Caribbean until Sunday. That left all of Saturday.

"Sounds like you have your plan," Emma said. She got up. "Off to bed, Wally. You too, Ariane. Tomorrow will be a big day."

Wally nodded. He looked at Ariane, hesitated, said, "Good night," and went out.

Ariane got ready for bed and climbed beneath the covers, but sleep eluded her for a long time.

◄◄ ►►

The proverb "it never rains but it pours" was unknown during Merlin's first lifetime on Earth, but during his second lifetime, in his new incarnation as Rex Major, he had observed its truth often enough.

The proverb usually referred to problems coming in swarms, and in his business dealings Major had seen that happen many times. On the magical side, though, he'd noticed that negative *and* positive things tended to happen in clumps.

It had nothing to do with coincidence, not when magic

was involved. Magic, after all, was simply a way to shape the world. It was all based on knowing the True Names of things: not Names in the sense of sounds that could be spoken out loud, but a deep, deep understanding of every aspect of the object's – or person's – makeup and internal workings. If you understood something, you could control it. If you understood it only partially, you could control it only partially. But if you understood it completely, you could control it completely.

In Faerie, magic was part of the natural order, a means of accomplishing things, a tool that everyone could use, though most managed only a very limited knowledge of True Names and thus had only minimal skill. On Earth, though, magic's influence was far greater, because it came from outside, subverting what humans liked to think of as immutable natural laws. On Earth, magic set in place *centuries* ago continued to tug at the strings of reality like a puppeteer manipulating a marionette.

So it did not surprise Rex Major, though it pleased him a great deal, that hard on the heels of the email telling him that the fourth shard of Excalibur had been sensed by the software that bore his magical imprint came an email telling him that his computer experts had found images of Ariane's mother online, placing her in Horseshoe Bay, B.C., just a couple of weeks previously.

Ariane's mother, Merlin knew, had been offered the power of the Lady of the Lake before Ariane had, and though she had rejected it, and then fled in a futile attempt to keep the magic from interfering with her daughter's life, she still bore magic within her. It continued to tug at her, as magic also tugged at Ariane and Wally and Felicia and even Merlin himself, the magic the Lady had infused into Excalibur and then set loose in this world to try to bring the shards of the sword together. Now the magic that wound around all those who had any connection to the sword was slowly tightening.

The sword wanted only to be whole. Merlin could not deny that it would prefer to be whole under the control of the Lady of the Lake – Ariane – but it would serve him, too, if he were the one who managed to forge it anew: its own strange sense of self-preservation burned brighter within it than the thin veneer of loyalty to its creator the Lady had attempted to lay upon it.

Major reached up to touch the ruby stud in his earlobe, caught himself doing it, and lowered his hand again. It was becoming a very bad habit, reaching for that jewel every time he thought of the sword – a "tell," as poker players would put it. Not that there was anyone to see, here in his office, to which he had returned after telling Felicia about their upcoming trip to the Caribbean. And where he had just hung up the phone after politely letting her parents know where she would be travelling, and strengthening the Commands that kept them from worrying about that fact. But even though there was no one to see him finger the stud at this moment, at some other time there might be, and it just might be someone who would realize what it meant.

He picked up the phone again. Horseshoe Bay, for all its seeming small-town-in-the-wilderness feel, was only fifteen kilometres from downtown Vancouver – and the offices of Excalibur Computer Systems.

CHAPTER SIX

HORSESHOE BAY

"AT LEAST IT'S NOT A SWIMMING POOL," Wally ventured.
After a good night's sleep – at least on his part; he wasn't sure about Ariane, who looked a little pale and bleary-eyed this morning – and a huge breakfast in the hotel's buffet restaurant, they had consulted a map of B.C. they'd found in the lodge lobby, and identified a likely place to travel to: Whyte Lake, a small body of fresh water about three kilometres inland from Horseshoe Bay. Of course, that meant it was tucked into a fold in a mountainside, but the map indicated a trail down.

A trail currently half-buried in snow. They'd checked the temperature on the Weather Network before they'd left for Horseshoe Bay: a predicted high of four degrees Celsius, a low of minus-three. Chilly, though a lot warmer than Saskatchewan.

But still cold enough for snow, and there'd obviously been quite a bit of it in the recent past. They stood on a floating wooden pier in the lake, after having clambered out of the near-freezing water and using Ariane's Patented Quick-Dry Method to avoid hypothermia. A sign indicated the path to the Baden-Powell Trail, which would take them down, according to the map, to a trailhead located in a small car park alongside the Trans-Canada Highway, just above Horseshoe Bay.

"It's not far," Ariane said. "And it's all downhill. Let's get going." She started off.

Wally sighed, and followed her along the pier and onto the alternately snowy-then-muddy trail. They passed an outhouse, and, after a short walk through the trees without encountering any difficulty, reached the spot where their path intersected with another, marked by an orange triangle attached to a tree bearing the letters BP in blue, a fleur-de-lis above it. An additional blue sign reiterated the fact they had reached the Baden-Powell Trail. Ariane and Wally turned left along it, and began picking their way downhill.

Although parts of the trail boasted boardwalks and wooden steps, parts didn't, and about ten minutes later, Wally was scooting down one particularly steep bit on his rear end, icy water soaking his bottom, his feet having slid out from under him twice before he gave up and decided indignity was preferable to infirmity. Sliding down the slope, he reflected once again on the fact that Saskatchewan people just didn't *do* mountains. And yet somehow he kept finding himself on slippery slopes.

Metaphorically as well as literally, perhaps. He wondered what waited for them at the bottom of the hill.

It turned out that the first thing that waited for them was Highway 99. The trail took them under it, then continued on a short distance to the Trans-Canada Highway. They heard it long before they reached it, as two motorcycles screamed by, one after the other, at what sounded like two hundred kilometres an hour.

They emerged at last into a small gravel parking lot that opened onto an access road; they followed that road a short distance, and then crossed onto a bridge that took them over the highway. The TransCanada ended at the B.C. Ferries terminal, and looking down from the bridge they could see cars lining up for the next ferry to Nanaimo.

Wally had been to Horseshoe Bay before; Ariane hadn't. But he didn't have a clue where the public library was, or even if there was one. In her backpack, Ariane carried the photo Wally had scanned to use in his Internet searches. She planned to show it around the waterfront businesses to see if anyone recognized her mom, while Wally did his thing on the Web – assuming he could find a computer.

Before they went into the town, though, he stopped and turned around and showed Ariane the soaked rear of his jeans. "Do you mind drying me off?" he said.

Ariane laughed. "Sorry. I already did that for myself." She whacked him playfully on the butt and he instantly felt warmer – in more ways than one. Ears burning, he set off along Marine Drive.

He didn't really know the town all that well, but he knew the bay lay downhill and to their right, so he turned down Nelson Drive, which seemed to go in pretty much the right direction. They walked along the tree- and hedge-lined street, past neat houses. They'd left the snow behind on the mountainside, it seemed: here, beneath grey skies, the roads were wet and cold mist shrouded everything, but only a little slush clung to life in the deepest shadows, looking as if it would rather have been anywhere else.

Nelson Drive, it turned out, delivered them to the end of the pier that stretched into the Bay, pointing like a finger at the giant ferry docked on the other side, the mist fading the ship from bright blue and white into the muted tones of an old photograph. A handful of boats nestled up to the docks on their side of the harbour, most of them buttoned down with awnings and tarpaulins. To their left, the mouth of the bay couldn't be seen in the mist, which also hid the glorious mountain views Wally remembered from his summertime visits.

But they weren't there for the scenery. And since he'd just had to slide down some of that scenery on his rear end, which, though it might no longer be damp, still felt decidedly bruised, he'd kind of had his fill of mountain scenery anyway.

They made their way through the park to Troll's, the restaurant that had been in the first photo of Ariane's mom Wally had uncovered. Just inside the front door, where framed caricatures of notable Canadians who had eaten there stared down from knotty-pine panelling, he asked the waitress who greeted them where he could find a public library. She blinked at him. "There's no public library in Horseshoe Bay," she said. "You'd have to go to West Vancouver."

Crap. "What about an Internet café?"

"No."

"*Anywhere* I could get onto a computer?"

The girl scratched her neck. "Just a second." She disappeared for a minute, came back. "Joe says he thinks there's a computer for guests staying at the Horseshoe Bay Motel. Just up the street a couple of blocks."

"Thanks." Wally turned to Ariane. "I'll go check it out. You're going to start asking around?"

Ariane nodded. She stared past him into the restaurant, at the handful of people enjoying breakfast – a rather late breakfast; they hadn't gotten away from Medicine Hat until late morning, and more than an hour had passed since they'd materialized in Whyte Lake. Even with the time difference, it was after 10 a.m. here. "It'd be an enormous stroke of luck to find her here," he said quietly.

"I know," Ariane said. "But she *was* here. That photo proved it. And not long ago. Maybe..."

Wally nodded. "Good luck," he said, and then, before he even knew he was going to do it, he leaned in and kissed her on the cheek as she had kissed him the night before.

Her eyes swung around to him, wide and slightly startled, and she raised a hand to her face.

He felt himself blushing, but he didn't look away. "We'll meet back here in an hour. Okay?"

"Okay."

He gave her a smile and a small wave, and stepped out of the restaurant.

The cool mist felt good on his burning ears.

◄◄ ►►

Ariane watched Wally go, hand still on her cheek. The waitress chuckled. "He's cute."

Ariane swung horrified eyes around to her. "Cute? Wally?"

"Sure," the waitress said. "He reminds me of my little brother. He used to be kind of gawky like that, but once he grew into his looks...these days he has to beat the girls off with a stick."

Ariane didn't know how to respond to that. She also didn't know how to respond to Wally's kiss. Sure, she'd kissed him first. But that had been a thank-you kiss. This had been a...a "see-you-later-girlfriend" kind of kiss. Were they really boyfriend and girlfriend now? She knew Wally was in love with her. She wasn't in love with him. Was she?

She hadn't decided. Did she have to decide now?

She shook her head to clear it. *No, not now. Later.*

"Table for one?" the waitress said.

Ariane gathered her wits. "No," she said. "I'm looking for someone. I know she eats here sometimes..." She shrugged out of her backpack and pulled her mom's photo out of an outside pocket. She held it out to the waitress. "Have you seen her?"

The waitress looked closely, but shook her head. "Sorry," she said. "So many people come and go here, what with the ferry terminal. Unless she's a local, she wouldn't make much of an impression."

"She *might* be living in town," Ariane said.

The waitress shook her head. "Sorry," she said again. Then her eyes slid past Ariane and her smile brightened. "Table for three?" she said to the man and woman and young girl who had just come in.

Ariane tucked the photo back into her backpack pocket and slunk outside into the cold mist. *Strike one*, she thought, but even if she got three strikes in a row, she wouldn't give up. Her mom had been in Horseshoe Bay. Someone must have seen her, have some idea of where she had gone. They had to. It couldn't be a dead end. It *couldn't*.

Except, of course, no matter how fervently she wished otherwise, it could.

But it isn't yet, she told herself fiercely. She looked up and down Bay Street. There were several restaurants and galleries and other businesses. She'd ask at every one. And then she'd go up a block and ask again. She'd ask until she ran out of places to ask. She wouldn't give up.

Someone in Horseshoe Bay had seen her mom, and Ariane wasn't leaving until she found that person.

She turned left and began her quest.

◄◄ ►►

The Horseshoe Bay Motel, its name emblazoned on a red awning in faux-Celtic letters, proved to be an old-fashioned two-storey motel with the room doors opening directly to the outside. Wally entered the small lobby, decorated with antique-looking furniture and West Coast-flavoured artwork. A rotund middle-aged woman sat behind the desk, reading the *Vancouver Sun.* She looked up as he came in and gave him a friendly smile. "Can I help you?"

"I heard you have a computer station," Wally said. "I wondered...could I use it?"

Her smile slipped a little. "Are you a guest?" she said.

"No," Wally said. "I'm catching the ferry later on. But I really need to use a computer." He gave her what he hoped was a winning smile. "My parents pulled me out of school early for a Christmas vacation trip out here but I forgot to get the homework I'd be missing from my teacher before I left. She said she'd email it to me, but I haven't had a chance to look. I wanted to work on it during the ferry ride."

It was a convoluted bit of make-believe, but it contained the magic words "parents" and "homework" and made him sound like a remarkably conscientious young man who clearly had no interest in, say, surfing for porn or playing video games on their precious computer.

He hoped.

The woman studied him for a moment. Then her smile came back. "Of course, dear," she said. She pointed to an alcove just off the lobby. "It's in there."

Wally went in, sat down at the office chair, and cracked his knuckles. Then he called up the website he'd used just a few weeks before to track Rex Major's flight to New Zealand. As far as he knew, Major had no idea that was how Wally had known where he was going. Even if he had, it wouldn't have mattered: if he was planning to fly to the Caribbean, his pilot had to file a flight plan. Even Rex Major had to obey *some* rules.

He still remembered the tail number from Major's private jet. A quick search, and there it was: Major was flying to – Wally frowned at the three-letter airport designation. It didn't mean anything to him. He called up a different site, did another search. The answer came back: Cacibajagua Island.

The name didn't mean any more to him than the airport designation had. But another quick Google took care of that.

Cacibajagua Island, it turned out, was a private island in the Caribbean, and a pretty remote one, a good three hours by boat from the Turks and Caicos. The island, owned by Cacibajagua Island Diving Adventures, featured a small but luxurious resort hotel, its own airfield, and most important, Jujo Cave: a spectacular sea cave which stretched for a full kilometre, its sinuous shape giving rise to its name, a Taino word for "snake." A mecca for cave divers, it was also, most unusually, accessible to non-divers and large enough that Cacibajagua Island Diving Adventures could pilot a small submarine along its entire length, although only during a three-hour window centred around high tide. At low tide parts of the cave partially emptied, the water in those chambers becoming too shallow for the sub to navigate.

Into the inland end of that cave poured a waterfall of fresh water. The photos of the "Cascade Chamber" were quite spectacular.

If the fourth shard of Excalibur were on that island, Wally was willing to bet it was hidden in that chamber. The freshwater cascade would have given the Lady easy access to it. If she had then simply slipped the shard beneath the cave's seawater, it would explain why Ariane hadn't sensed it. As for how *Rex Major* had located it... *Some pesky diver*, Wally thought. *I wonder if a smartphone can be made waterproof enough so a diver can use it for an underwater camera?*

A quick Google for the terms "waterproof smartphone

for divers" showed that, indeed, it could be.

That's it. The fourth shard has to be there. And thanks to Ariane, we can get there before Rex Major.

He checked the time on the computer screen: past 11 a.m. His hour was up. Time to find Ariane and tell her the good news.

Wally left the alcove, smiled his thanks at the desk clerk, and exited into the parking lot. But as he turned toward Roy Street his heart leaped into his throat.

A black SUV had just rolled past in the direction of the bay, and on the side of it had been emblazoned a golden sword and the letters ECS.

Excalibur Computer Systems!

Wally set off down Roy Street at a run.

CHAPTER SEVEN

AN OLD BRIDGE AND AN OLD MAN

WALLY HAD BEEN GONE for almost an hour and Ariane had tried every business along Bay Street without success. Her last hope was the Spirit Gallery just a couple of doors down from Troll's; it had been closed when she'd gone by it the first time, with a "Back in 15 Minutes" sign on the door. Noting that the sign was gone, she ducked inside.

The walls were hung with amazing work by West Coast native artists, and Ariane wished she had time to browse – not that she'd be buying anything, as her first glimpse of a price tag made clear, unless it was a T-shirt – but Wally would be looking for her in a few minutes. The young woman behind the glass-topped display counter filled with jewelry at the centre of the gallery smiled at her as she came in. "Did you try to stop in earlier?" she said. "I thought I saw you as I was coming down the street. I'd just run out to get my coffee mug refilled." She indicated a red travel mug by the counter. "It's been such a slow day I didn't expect anyone to come in. I'm glad you came back."

Ariane felt a little badly, since she wasn't really a customer. *Maybe I can find something to take home as a souvenir*, she told her conscience. *Now, stop bothering me.* "Actually, I'm looking for someone." Ariane held out her mother's photo, more out of a sense of duty than hope. "I know she was in Horseshoe Bay for at least a few days a couple of weeks ago. Did you happen to see her?"

The woman looked at the photo. "Are you with the two men who were down at the other end of the street?"

Ariane's heart quickened. "What?"

"In the coffee shop, two men were asking Tracy Hoffman if she'd seen the same woman."

Rex Major's men! They must be! "What did she say?" she said, trying to keep her voice from shaking.

"That she bought coffee and a muffin last Saturday before boarding the late afternoon ferry to Nanaimo."

"She's left town?" Disappointment struck like a blow. "Days ago?"

"Oh, yes." The woman gave Ariane a curious look. "Friend of yours?"

"A...relative," Ariane said. "An aunt. I've lost track of her. I have some...family news."

"Really?" the woman said. She suddenly sounded suspicious. "Because as it happens, before she went to Tracey's she spent quite a long time in here. She didn't buy anything but she was very interested in the art. We had a long chat. She told me she didn't *have* any family."

"Family issues," Ariane said, thinking quickly. "She didn't get along with my mother. Look, it's all kind of private..."

"Oh, of course," the woman said, blushing a little. "I didn't mean to pry."

"Did...did she say anything about what she was going to do in Nanaimo?"

"Oh, she wasn't staying in Nanaimo," the woman said. "She was going to catch a bus down to Victoria."

"Did she say why?"

"She said she had a job lined up at the Empress."

Ariane blinked. "The Empress?"

The woman laughed. "The Fairmont Empress. The big old CP hotel in Victoria. Looks like a castle, right down on the waterfront?"

Ariane's hopes, which had fallen so hard a moment before, lifted again. "You're sure?"

"That's what she said."

"Did...did, um...Tracey...say anything about that to those two men?"

"Tracey didn't know. She just knew she was getting on the Nanaimo ferry."

We're still one step ahead, Ariane thought. "Those men may come talk to you, too," she said carefully. "Would you do me a favour, and not tell them you heard my...aunt...say she was going to Victoria? To this...Empress? I can't explain, but my...aunt...really doesn't want them to find her."

"But does she want *you* to find her?" the woman said.

"She doesn't know I'm looking for her," Ariane said.

The woman looked at her closely. "She's not really your aunt, is she?"

Ariane felt something close to panic. "What? Yes! I –"

"No, there's no way. You hesitate every time you call her that. And this photo..." She pointed to it, still lying on the counter between them, "tells a different story. You're the spitting image of her. She's your mother, isn't she?"

"We just...it's just a family resemblance...we..." Ariane's voice trailed off. The woman clearly didn't believe her. "Yes," she said quietly. "She's my mom. She disappeared two years ago. I don't know why." Not quite true – she knew it had something to do with the Lady of the Lake revealing herself to her mother and offering her the same power and quest Ariane had since accepted, but she didn't think bringing living Arthurian legends into the conversation would do much to convince the woman of her truthfulness. "I've been looking for her."

She watched the woman's face, wondering how she'd react. To her relief, she saw only sympathy. "I thought it must be something like that," she said. "And the two men?"

"Private detectives, I think," Ariane said, stepping away from the glaring light of the truth into the comfortable shadows of falsehood. "Mom owed a lot of money when she vanished."

"Probably *why* she vanished," the woman said. She regarded Ariane for a moment then pushed her mom's photo back over the glass countertop. "I won't tell them about the job in Victoria," she said. "If they ask me. But you know they'll find her eventually, if they're this close. Nobody can just vanish in this day and age. You'd have to be magic to manage it."

"Thank you," Ariane said. To her horror she found tears in her eyes. "Thank you," she mumbled again, and busied herself returning the photo to its waterproof plastic bag, and the bag to the pocket of her backpack.

"You're welcome, hon," the woman said, her voice warm with sympathy. "Good luck. I hope you find her. I hope she's glad to see you when you do."

"Me, too," Ariane said. "Thank you again." She gave a tentative wave, then turned and hurried out onto the sodden, misty street. She looked both ways. She didn't see the two men, but she did see Wally, dashing around the corner of Troll's. She ran toward him.

"Rex Major –"

"Rex Major –"

They'd spoken at the same instant. They stopped at the same instant, and stared at each other. "Rex Major's men are here," Wally panted. "I saw an SUV with the Excalibur Computer Systems logo on it."

"They're looking for Mom," Ariane said. "They had a

photo. They knew she'd been here. And they know she left on the ferry for Nanaimo a week ago."

"We can get to Nanaimo first," Wally said.

Ariane shook her head. "Not Nanaimo. Victoria."

Wally's eyebrows lifted. "Victoria? You know something they don't?"

"I hope so," Ariane said.

Wally looked up at the overcast sky. "Well, perfect weather for it, don't you think?"

"Perfect," Ariane said. "But not here. In case someone is watching. Let's go into the park."

They crossed the street. On a sunny summer day the park that bordered the bay would have been full of tourists. On a grey, foggy December day, it was deserted. Ariane reached out her hand to Wally. He took it.

Car doors slammed. Someone shouted. Ariane jerked her head around to see two men running toward them, men in dark suits, a black SUV parked haphazardly on the street, its doors still open.

Then Ariane let the power of the Lady and the shard of Excalibur she carried fill her, and together she and Wally leaped into the clouds.

◄◄ ►►

Despite all the times he'd done it, Wally still hated the sensations of travelling via the Lady's power. Oh, sure, it sounded like fun, dissolving into nothingness and zipping around in the clouds or streams, but in fact – and he wasn't ashamed to admit it, at least to himself, if not to Ariane – a part of him gibbered in terror every time. In classic *Star Trek* episodes, every one of which he'd watched at least twice (along with all its later incarnations – *Next Generation, Deep Space Nine, Voyager,* even *Star Trek: Enterprise*), Dr. McCoy occasionally complained about the whole beam-me-up-Scotty-disintegration-reintegration method of transportation, calling it unnatural. Wally sympathized.

He could always feel Ariane with him, his brain – or spirit or whatever remained intact – interpreting her presence as her still holding his hand. He occasionally wondered what would happen if she somehow released his "hand" while they were in the mysterious magical pipeline to wherever they were headed. Then he tried really hard to stop wondering about it, because he had a good enough imagination that the thought occasionally gave him nightmares.

He didn't understand how his brain could even keep working when it had no body: it offended all his scientific sensibilities. But everything that had happened since the Lady of the Lake had shown up in Wascana Lake had offended his scientific sensibilities, so he supposed he should be used to it.

One thing he could never tell was how much time had passed. He couldn't see anything, or hear anything, and insomuch as he felt anything, it was like floating in a sensory deprivation tank – not that he'd ever done such a thing, but he'd read about it. All he knew was that the world went away around him – and then it came back.

As usual, it came back cold and wet.

"Pfah." He surged upward in cold water and spat some from his mouth. It tasted awful. Ariane stood beside him, chest-deep beneath the stone arch of a bridge. He figured Ariane had chosen the spot because it provided some shelter and minimized the chance someone would see them suddenly pop into existence out of nowhere.

He looked farther afield. They were in a shallow, clearly artificial lake, the bridge arching over a narrow spot in its middle. To their left, water sprayed from an aeration fountain like a giant lawn sprinkler, redundantly watering the water. To their right, evergreen trees poked up, spiky and green, from a small island. Bushes and trees grew on their side of the lake, while the other sides looked very open. The mist that had shrouded Horseshoe Bay clung to everything here as well, so that the buildings surrounding the park at some distance loomed grey and indistinct.

Ariane turned and led the way out from under the bridge to the left. They stayed close to the stone wall until they could finally clamber up the muddy bank into a screen of bushes. There Ariane dried them off, and then at last they could stroll out onto the path like any other pair of teens. They walked up onto the old stone bridge.

"Victoria, I presume," Wally said.

Ariane nodded. "But I don't know exactly where we are."

"Shouldn't be hard to figure out," Wally said. "It's a park. There'll be a sign...somewhere." They'd reached the middle of the bridge they'd just climbed out from under like a pair of trolls. *And we were just at Troll's in Horseshoe Bay*, he thought, his mouth twitching into a smile of private amusement. *I think it's a theme.* He stopped and looked around, and then down. A metal plaque right in front of them read, "Stone Bridge. This rustic stone medieval bridge was constructed in 1889, as part of John Blair's landscape design for Beacon Hill Park."

"I think we're in Beacon Hill Park," he said.

"Thank you, Sherlock."

"Elementary, my dear Watson."

"Except that still doesn't help. I have no idea where Beacon Hill Park is in relation to the Empress."

"The Empress?" Wally blinked. "Why do we need to go there... Oh," he interrupted himself, feeling an odd sensation in his stomach, a momentary surge of excitement followed by a sinking feeling. "You should know," he said, "that when I called my dad last night, he told me he's in Victoria. And he's staying at the Empress."

Ariane's eyes widened. "Maybe he could help!" she said excitedly. "He might have seen Mom, if she's working there. Or he could talk to the management for us. They'd listen to him, he's a grownup, a businessman..." Her voice trailed off, her excitement dying as his had a moment before and, he was certain, for the same reason: she'd realized that however nice it would be to let a grownup take charge, this *particular* grownup wouldn't do. "No, that won't work, will it?"

"No," Wally said. "In fact, it complicates things. We have to make sure he doesn't see us. He's under Merlin's Command. He must be. It's the only way Dad would be willing to let Flish live in Rex Major's condo *and* let him fly her off to the Caribbean for a scuba-diving adventure, of all things."

Ariane blinked. "Scuba diving? What?"

Wally realized he hadn't had a chance to tell her yet what he'd found out on the computer in the Horseshoe Bay Motel. So while they stood in the mist in the middle of the "medieval" bridge, watching the aerating fountain endlessly spray water into the air, he told her about Cacibajagua Island, Rex Major's Caribbean destination. "There's a big cave called Joju," he said. "It's hundreds of metres long. Inland, it ends in a chamber that's mostly filled with salt water at high tide, but empties out quite a bit at low tide. There's a freshwater waterfall that pours into that chamber. Can you think of a better place for the Lady to have hidden a shard of Excalibur? Or a better reason why you can't sense it than that it's submerged beneath salt water?"

"It makes perfect sense," Ariane agreed, grinning with excitement. "When will Major and Flish get there?"

"The flight plan has them taking off tomorrow morning.

It's only a three-hour flight. They'll be there before noon Toronto time."

"Then we have to get there first."

Wally said nothing. He'd already done the math. Clearly Ariane was coming to the same conclusion he had. He saw her smile dissolve into a worried frown, and wished he could wipe it away. "That means we only have today to look for Mom!" She stared around into the fog. "We have to find the Empress!"

"Guess we'd better ask directions," Wally said. "I've been to Victoria, but I've never been in Beacon Hill Park. Come on."

He led Ariane across the bridge. Together they walked along the edge of the lake until they came to a paved foot-path through dripping tall trees around the same end of the lake where the aeration fountain sprayed. There they met an old man with a cane, taking a slow constitutional through the mist in a heavy overcoat and muffler, a fur hat jammed rather haphazardly on his head. "Excuse me," Wally said politely. "Can you point us in the direction of the Fairmont Empress?"

The old man squinted up at him, an amused quirk to his mouth. "You misplace it?"

"Kind of," Wally said.

The old man snorted. "Never heard of anyone losing something that big before." He turned and pointed back the way he'd come. "You go up Arbutus Way to the edge of the park, turn left along Southgate. At the traffic light turn right onto Douglas – take the left fork, not the right. One more block and you'll see the Empress off to your left."

"How far?" Ariane said.

"About a half a mile." Wally was still trying to convert that in his head when the old man, clearly sensing his con-fusion, sighed and said, "Less than a kilometre, I mean." He shook his head. "Never heard of anyone losing the

Empress. Not this close to it."

"We're from Saskatchewan," Wally said.

The old man laughed. "Aren't we all?" He poked a thumb in his chest. "Fifty years in Moose Jaw. Go Riders!" With a grin and friendly wave, he resumed his walk into the park.

Wally and Ariane went the other way, following the old man's instructions, and within a few minutes the Empress hove into sight, like a vast ship anchored at the head of the harbour. Wally had seen it before, but Ariane stopped and stared when they could finally see it all. "Wow," she said. "And your dad is staying there?"

Wally nodded. His eyes flicked over the grounds. They weren't nearly as overrun with tourists as when he'd been there with his family in the summertime, but there were still plenty of people around. Behind them, as they stood at the corner of Belleville and Government Streets, rose the tower of the Centennial Carillon in front of the Royal B.C. Museum. The B.C. Legislature, looking even grimmer and greyer than usual, loomed in the mist a few hundred metres to their left.

"Must be nice," Ariane said.

She kept standing there, staring at the hotel. As if the mist weren't cold and wet enough, a light drizzle began to fall. Wally shivered. And still Ariane didn't move. "Are we going in?" he said at last.

"What?" She glanced at him, surprised, as if she'd forgotten he was there. "Sorry." She took a deep breath. "Keep an eye out for your father."

"I will," Wally said. "But he's probably not in the hotel this time of day. Off doing...whatever he's doing here."

"What *does* he do?" Ariane said, turning her gaze back toward the hotel.

"He's a management consultant. Whatever that is."

Ariane nodded, but he didn't think she'd really heard

him. "All right," she said. She hitched her backpack higher. "Here goes nothing." She strode toward the castle-like hotel.

Wally trailed behind her, wondering what she was thinking, what she was feeling, what would happen if she found her mother – and what would happen if she didn't.

The fourth shard still waited in the Caribbean – *if* their guess was correct – and they were running out of time.

At least it'll be warm and dry in the hotel, he thought, and quickened his steps to catch up.

CHAPTER EIGHT

TEA AT THE EMPRESS

Now that she was potentially so close to finding her mom, Ariane found herself strangely reluctant to take the next step. But she and Wally couldn't stand in the drizzle forever, so at last she hitched her backpack higher on her shoulders – unnecessarily, but it had that feeling of getting ready for battle – and set off.

Although just whom she thought she'd have to battle, she didn't know.

She didn't say anything to Wally, but part of the reason she hesitated was that the shard of Excalibur she wore strapped to her skin seemed...uneasy. If that made sense when you were talking about an ancient iron fragment. But of course it did make sense when that ancient iron fragment was part of something which, if not exactly sentient, certainly had its own desires, and its own strange links to the Lady of the Lake, who had forged it, and to Arthur, who had wielded it – both of whose heirs were, here and now, trudging along the sidewalk toward the towering old hotel, its façade overgrown with ivy almost to the copper-clad roof.

The hotel's name, The Empress, was written in ivy-wreathed, elegant italicized capitals above what had once been the grand entrance, but the current main doors were further along, up the curving drive. A bronze statue of Captain James Cook glared at them with seeming disapproval from the other side of Government Street as they splashed past him through rain that was growing heavier by the minute.

When they entered the lobby, Ariane started to order them dry – then didn't. The staff could hardly fail to notice, and that was the kind of anomaly they might happily share with Rex Major's minions, if and when they traced Ariane's mom this far.

The lobby was white and pillared, centred by a giant flower vase atop a round table of dark wood surrounded by a Persian rug, and lit by a skylight three stories above. It might have intimidated Ariane if she weren't so focussed on the strange sensations from the shard – could a piece of sword blade actually *squirm?* Because that was what it felt like. Her pulse raced as she confronted the possibility she might actually be close to finding her mom. She stopped by the flower vase and shrugged out of her backpack.

"Why are we still wet?" Wally complained.

"Because I don't want to draw any special attention," Ariane said. She dug the plastic bag containing her mom's picture out of the backpack pocket, and pulled out the photo. "Here goes nothing," she said. Heart now pounding as if she'd run a marathon, she walked up to the front desk, carrying the backpack loose in her left hand.

The young Japanese woman behind the counter smiled at her. "May I help you?" she said. She had a slight accent.

Ariane held out the photo. "I'm looking for this woman," she said, her mouth dry even as she dripped on the carpet. "Someone said she started working here...probably just this week."

The woman looked down at the photo. "Oh, yes," she said. "You're in luck. I met her just yesterday. Nice lady. She's working in the Tea Lobby. In fact, she should be there now: the first service started at 11:30."

"The...Tea Lobby?" Ariane said, even as the thumping of her heart threatened to drown out all other sounds. *Mom...here...today...in this building!*

The last time she'd seen her mother had been a few days after that dreadful night when Emily Forsythe had staggered back to the house from her walk around the lake and collapsed on the front step, wet and raving. In the psych ward at the Regina General Hospital, she had yelled and screamed and claimed Ariane wasn't her daughter, that she didn't have a daughter. And then, somehow, she'd escaped from the ward and disappeared.

There'd been no word from her ever since. Nothing. Nothing at all, while Ariane drifted from foster home to foster home until Aunt Phyllis finally took her in. Ariane's family, her happiness, had all been stripped away from her. Ariane now knew – or thought she knew – that her mom had seen the Lady of the Lake; that her mom had been offered the same quest: to find the shattered shards of Excalibur before Merlin – Rex Major – could do so; that her mom had refused the power and then had fled to try to protect Ariane. To no avail, as it turned out.

But now that she faced the imminent possibility of seeing her mom again, she realized something she had never allowed herself to realize before: while, yes, she longed to talk to her mother, she was also angry.

In fact, she was furious.

The sword continued to squirm against her flank, burning hot one instant, cold as ice the next. She had to clench her fists to keep her hands from shaking.

"You take the stairs over there," the young woman said, pointing across the lobby, "to the upstairs lobby – then it's just straight down the hallway that way." She pointed the opposite direction. "You can't miss it."

"Thank you," Ariane said.

She turned and walked across the Persian rug to the broad curving staircase the woman had indicated, Wally following her. Halfway up the stairs, out of sight of the front desk, she suddenly got tired of being wet and let the magic dry them both. But the sword blazed as she did it, and the water didn't just spray, it burst from them in a blast of steam.

"Whoa," Wally said, as they reached the top of the stairs. "A little tense?"

Ariane said nothing. Fists still clenched, she stalked across the upper lobby to the hallway leading to the Tea Lobby.

While the main lobby was refined in a modern sort of way, the corridor they now entered, with its dark wood and palm fronds, evoked Victorian England. The sound of a pianist playing "As Time Goes By" drifted toward them as they approached the Tea Lobby, which was set off by chest-high barriers made to look like old-fashioned, small-paned windows with frosted glass. With Wally trailing behind, she walked up to the barriers and looked into the elegant space beyond. More Persian rugs covered a wooden parquet floor. White pillars reached up to a ceiling crisscrossed by beams of carved, dark wood. Heavy red and gold drapes, open to let in the grey light, framed windows that looked out onto the front lawn and, beyond Government Street, the Inner Harbour.

She saw her mother at once, near the far end of the Tea Lobby, wearing a long-sleeved white blouse and an elegant red vest.

Mom looked older than Ariane remembered; older than two years could account for. She'd lost weight, and her face had a slightly haggard look Ariane had never seen when she still lived at home. But when she smiled at two old ladies in big pink hats, leaning down to offer sweets, she smiled the same smile Ariane remembered, the one she had loved so much.

Her mom didn't see Ariane rounding the dividers and walking toward her. But her smile faltered as she straightened; and then, without any warning at all, she simply collapsed. The china plates from the serving stand smashed on the floor, a single cookie rolling away as though trying to flee the disaster. The elderly ladies screamed. Other servers turned and stared.

Ariane broke into a run.

She reached her mom's side in an instant. Her mother's eyes were closed, but her head turned this way and that, restlessly, and she moaned, "No, no, take it away, take it away..."

Another of the servers, a black man with white hair, grabbed Ariane's shoulders and pulled her away from her mom. "Give her air, give her air," he said, and turned and spread his arms wide to keep any other gawkers from approaching.

Ariane wanted to lash out at him, wanted to cry, *She's my mother!* But suddenly she understood what had happened, why her mother had collapsed, and in horror she turned and ran the other way, back into the hallway.

Wally hadn't moved. He stared at her, his face white, freckles standing out on it. "What happened?"

"It's the shard," Ariane gasped. "The shard – she can't bear to be around it. And it doesn't want to be around her, either." Heedless of the stares of a passing couple, she jerked her shirt out of the waistband of her jeans, reached inside it and undid the tensor bandage that held the first shard of Excalibur, the one they'd found in the Northwest Territories, against her skin. Its mate still lay beneath the mattress of her bed at Barringer Farm. She held it out to

Wally. "Take it!"

Wally hesitated only an instant, then pulled it to him and stuffed it into his pocket.

Without another word, Ariane turned and ran back to her mother.

She wasn't lying on the floor anymore. Instead, she was sitting up, her back to one of the white pillars. "I'm sorry, Jim," she was saying to the black man, "I don't know what came...over..."

Her voice trailed to silence as she saw Ariane.

The two of them stared at each other for a long moment. Ariane found she didn't know what to say, and wouldn't have been able to say it if she did. Her throat had seized up, constricted by the tsunamis of conflicting emotions pouring through her. She wanted to hug her mother. She wanted to swear at her. She wanted to run away. She wanted to never leave again. In the end, she just stood there and waited for her mom to do something.

"The nurse is on her way," Jim said. "You just wait here."

"No," Ariane's mom said. "I'm fine. Really." She struggled to her feet, Jim lurching forward to help her when he realized what she was about to do. She pushed his hands gently away and stood on her own. "See?" She smiled at the elderly ladies she'd been serving, whose wide, worried eyes stared at her from beneath the brims of their hats. "I'm sorry if I frightened you."

"Don't mention it, dear," one of them said.

"You might want to see a doctor," the other said. "You might be pregnant."

Ariane's mom laughed. The sound, so familiar, so forgotten, pierced Ariane's heart like a dagger. "I don't think so," her mom said. But the smile fled as she turned to face her daughter again. They still hadn't spoken to each other, and her mom didn't speak now: instead, she just inclined her head toward a corner of the room, at an empty table by the big fireplace, right up against the windows over-looking the Inner Harbour, then turned to Jim. "I'll just have a sit-down over there in the corner with my young...niece, here," she said lightly. "You can send the nurse over when he arrives."

Jim seemed to really notice Ariane for the first time: "Your niece?" he said. He looked closely at her for a moment, then his face split into a big smile. "Ah, yes, I see the resemblance." He held out his hand. "Very glad to meet you, Miss...?"

"Felicia," Ariane said. She didn't want to give her own name and Wally's sister's was the first that popped into her head.

"Felicia," Jim said.

"Flish for short," Ariane said, just because she could.

"Flish," Jim corrected. He indicated the corner table. "Well, Flish, you sit right over there and keep an eye on your aunt." Jim turned back to the small crowd that had gathered. "Everything's fine, ladies and gentlemen," he said loudly. "I apologize for the disturbance. Please, return to your tea."

Ariane's mom walked over to the corner table without looking back at her daughter, sat, and *still* didn't look at her, instead staring out at the misty grey harbour. Captain Cook still looked unhappy, Ariane noted as she sat down across the table from her mom, her heart pounding again. "Mom?" she whispered finally, her throat so tight she could barely get even that single strangled syllable to pass through it.

"Oh, Ariane," her mom said, still looking out at the harbour. "What have you done?"

"I found you," Ariane said. "I..."

"You took the power," Emily Forsythe said. And now, at last, she turned. Tears glimmered in her eyes, left glistening tracks as they spilled down her cheeks. "You took the Lady's power. *How could you?"*

"I..." Ariane didn't know how to explain. "Merlin...he had to be –"

"You've made him your enemy," Ariane's mom said. "You've made him *our* enemy." She suddenly leaned forward and took Ariane's hand. Her heart thumped at the touch. She'd longed for that touch for so many long, lonely months. "I refused the power because I knew that was what would happen," her mom said. "I ran away because I didn't want Rex Major to find out about you, to come after you. I gave up my life, *our* life, to protect you...and you threw all that away. *Why?"*

Every word seemed to twist the blade her mom's laugh had first plunged into her heart. She'd never imagined this: never imagined she would find her mother, and her mom wouldn't be happy about it...would be angry. Angry with *her.*

Then her own anger kindled. Just a spark, but even though she was not wearing the shard, had left it with Wally out in the hallway – she hadn't turned to see, but she was certain he must be watching them – the sword's power fanned it instantly to a bright, hot flame. She jerked her hand free. "You want to know why I took the power?" Ariane almost snarled. "I took it because my mother abandoned me when I was *thirteen years old!* I took it because I'd been raised by strangers for *two years!* I took it because I was in trouble and being bullied! *Again!*

She heard herself becoming loud, saw heads turning their way. She reined herself in. "I took it to protect myself. I took it to protect the world. But the main reason I took it was because I thought it would help me find you. Now I have. And now I find out you don't even want me here." She heard her voice rising again, knew people were staring, but she didn't care. "You probably never wanted me. That's why you really left, wasn't it? Your daughter turned into a teenager and you didn't want to have to deal with *that!* So you ran way, just like my father did when I was born!"

Mom's face went white. "Ariane, no..." She reached out, but Ariane snatched her hands off the table.

She couldn't sit there anymore. She stood up. "I'm sorry I found you, I'm sorry I'm such a disappointment to you. But I'm not sorry I took the power. I'm going to complete the quest you refused. I'm going to get every shard of Excalibur. I'm going to see the sword remade, and I'm going to drive Merlin back into Faerie where he belongs. And then maybe...*maybe*...I'll come looking for you again."

It was a great exit line. She had every intention of turning and stalking coldly away after delivering it. But before she could her mother surged out of her chair, rounded the table, grabbed her, and pulled her into an all-encompassing embrace.

Ariane stiffened, arms straight at her sides. She heard her mother's sobs, felt her body shaking – and then she felt something else: a connection, a tingle of power she recognized.

Her mother might have rejected the Lady's offer, but the blood of the Lady – the line of magic stretching back unbroken to the days of King Arthur – still ran in her mother's veins as it did in her own, and Ariane could sense it. She hadn't, until the hug, but now it was as if a thread had been strung from her mother to herself, a gossamer-thin but unbreakable connection. The sensation made her gasp, and helped drive back the Excalibur-fuelled portion of her anger. That left her own seething cauldron of emotions, and though anger was part of that bubbling mix, it was only a small part. The largest part was still love – and it was love which brought her arms up and around her mother at last, and made that thin thread of connection between them thicken and thrum with sudden power.

"Do you feel that?" Mom gasped.

"I do," Ariane said. Tears had started in her eyes, and once more made it hard to speak. "Oh, Mom, I do."

They stood like that for a long moment. At last Emily Forsythe released her daughter and stepped back. She put her hands on Ariane's shoulders. "You've grown," she said. Tears still glistened in her eyes and on her cheeks. "As tall as I am, now."

It was true. Ariane hadn't registered it until that moment. Her own eyes filled anew. *Two years.* "Taller, I think." She brushed at her eyes. "Mom, I'm sorry. What I just said. I –"

"I deserved it," her mom said. "I know I hurt you. I..." She looked up. "Here's the staff nurse," she said in a falsely bright voice. "Hi, John."

"Hi, Emily." John, a small, wiry young man, shorter than Ariane *or* her mom, wore a pale blue golf shirt, black trousers and black shoes. Aside from a nametag reading "John McIntyre, R.N.," there was nothing to indicate he was a nurse, unless it was the black doctor's bag he carried. "You don't look sick, but Jim said you fainted?"

"I'm sure it's nothing," Emily said. "I didn't sleep well last night, so I overslept this morning, which means I skipped breakfast, and I've been on my feet all day."

"Hmmm." John looked at Ariane, and gave her a professionally friendly smile. "And who's this?"

"My niece...." Ariane's mom began, then hesitated.

"Felicia," Ariane said. "I haven't seen Aunt Emily in a long time."

"And you just happened to show up when she fainted?"

Ariane nodded. "Scared me half to death," she said truthfully.

"Hmmm," John said again. He turned to Emily. "Any other symptoms? Palpitations? Previous dizzy spells? Have you been sick recently?"

"No, no, no, and no," Emily said, ticking off each negative by bending down a finger on her left hand. That left her with a closed fist with thumb extended, which she turned into a big thumbs-up.

John laughed. "I'll just check your blood pressure," he said.

While John got out a stethoscope and wrapped the cuff of the blood-pressure machine around her mom's upper left arm, Ariane finally looked back toward the hallway. As she'd suspected, Wally stood there, looking worried. She gave him her mom's thumbs-up signal, and he smiled – but only slightly. He held up his wrist and tapped his watch. She knew what he meant: their time here was limited. Every minute they spent in Victoria was one less minute they'd have in the Caribbean to look for the shard.

But she ignored the signal and turned back to her mother.

John finished reading her mom's blood pressure and opened his bag again to stow away the stethoscope and the...the... "What do you call those things?" Ariane asked.

John looked up at her. "Hmmm?"

"The blood-pressure thingie. What's the scientific name?"

"Sphygmomanometer," John said. He grinned. "Why? You thinking of becoming a nurse...or a doctor?"

"It's crossed my mind," Ariane said, which earned her a startled look from her mother.

"Good for you." John straightened. "Blood pressure is normal, pulse is good, your colour is good, I don't think there's anything to worry about. But if it happens again, you should see your doctor."

"I will, John. Thank you."

"Don't mention it." John gave a friendly wave to Ariane,

and went off to talk to Jim, who was hovering near one of the pillars, watching them.

Ariane sat down again across from the table from her mother. "A doctor?" her mom said quizzically. "Last I heard, you wanted to be a ballerina."

"That was when I was seven," Ariane said. "And I haven't taken dance lessons since you disappeared."

Ariane's mom's face fell. "Oh," she said softly. "I'm sorry, Ariane. I'm so sorry this happened to us. To both of us. But you have to believe me. I thought I was doing the right thing. I didn't know the Lady would offer you the power, too. I thought that if I left, I'd take the power with me, that you'd be safe from it, and from Rex Major."

"I believe you," Ariane said, and despite all the harsh things she'd said before, it was true. But it didn't change the hurt and heartache of the past two years. And it didn't change the facts now. "But none of us are safe, Mom. Not as long as Rex Major is still after the sword."

"But with the power..." Her mom glanced around, then leaned in closer and lowered her voice. "I felt it when I hugged you. I can still feel it. You've got so much power, Ariane. It was like hugging a giant battery. What can you do with it?"

"I can...use water," Ariane said. "Shape it and wield it like a tool or a weapon. I can travel through water...fresh water, not salt."

"But how could you use that power to get here?" Emily Forsythe said. "We're on an island."

"I can fly, kind of," Ariane said. "Through the clouds."

Her mom's eyes widened. "Is it dangerous?"

"No," Ariane lied. Because of course it was – everything about the power of the Lady was dangerous. Always there was that seductive urge to let go, to dissolve into nothingness in stream or cloud. And if she ever ran out of power before she could safely materialize...She remembered barely saving herself on the crossing back from France after Wally's betrayal by plunging into the swimming pool of a fortuitous cruise ship.

"And I'm not travelling alone," she added. "I have a friend with me. He's over there by those window-things at the entrance."

"I figured he was with you," Mom said dryly. "We don't get a lot of teenage boys hanging around the Tea Lobby hoping for a chance at a few crumpets." She raised a hand and waved at Wally, gesturing for him to join them.

"Mom, no!" Ariane jumped up and waved Wally back. Since he hadn't moved, that was easy.

"But I want to meet him," Mom said.

"I *want* you to meet him," Ariane said. She lowered her voice in turn. "But not while he's carrying one of the shards of Excalibur. That's what made you faint."

Mom blinked. "What?"

"What did you feel, just before you passed out?"

Her mother frowned, thinking. "Everything was normal, and then there was this weird feeling, like something was pushing me away – not physically, but my consciousness – pushing it out of my body...you think that was the sword?"

"I think so," Ariane said. "Mom, I don't understand the Lady's power any more than you do, even though I've got so much more of it. But..." She hesitated. "I think the Lady is the right one for us to be allied with, but I don't think for a minute she's entirely friendly. Or kind. I think...I *know*...she was angry that you refused her. That anger bled over into the power she gave me. I felt it a minute ago. What I said...that wasn't me."

Not entirely, she inwardly qualified, but didn't say it. "A lot of that anger came from the sword. When a piece of it came close to you, I think it tried to punish you, to strike you down. It's not a complete sword, but it's still a weapon. It did what it could to you. If Wally comes any closer, it could happen again."

Ariane's mom let out a low whistle. "We really aren't in Kansas anymore, are we?"

"No."

Jim came over the table. "I think you should take the rest of the day off, Emily," he said. "The nurse says he doesn't think there's anything too much wrong with you, but after fainting..."

"Thanks, Jim," Emily said with a smile.

"I'll let your niece look after you." Jim grinned at Ariane. Ariane smiled back. Jim went away. But then Ariane had to turn back to her mom and tell her the truth.

"I can't stay," she said.

Her mom's face fell. "What? But –"

"I can't tell you too much." *I don't* want *to tell you too much,* Ariane thought. *For your own safety.* "Wally and I have to go somewhere else, right away. We're after the fourth shard of Excalibur and we think Rex Major knows where it is. We have to get to it before he does."

"Ariane..." her mom said, worry in her voice. "This is exactly what I was trying to avoid. By accepting the power of the Lady, you've put yourself in danger."

"I know," Ariane said. "And I've put you in danger, too." She took a deep breath. "Rex Major's men were in Horseshoe Bay this morning, just like we were. They know you took the ferry to Nanaimo. I don't think they know you took a job at the Empress, but they might. You've got to leave, without telling anyone where you're going."

"I *can't,*" Mom said. "Ariane, I have to eat. I have to have a place to live. And that means I have to work. I don't have any money saved up, not anymore. I took out everything I could when I...ran away, but it's all gone. It's been gone for quite a while. I was at my wit's end when I got this job. I've only been here a week. I can't just quit."

"But Rex Major's men –"

"How did you find out I was here?"

"A lady...in that First Nations art gallery in Horseshoe Bay. The one right down on Bay Street."

"Did she tell Rex Major's men?"

"No," Ariane said. "She hadn't talked to them. And she promised me she wouldn't tell them anything if she did."

"Well, then," her mom said. "I didn't tell anyone else, I swear. They can trace me to Nanaimo but they'll never trace me here."

"You took a bus."

"Actually, I didn't. I got a ride with a nice woman I met on the ferry. I didn't tell her my real name. We got in her car down on the car deck, quite early, before most of the crowds came down. Nobody saw me. There's no way they'll be able to trail me down here."

"Rex Major has men in Victoria, too," Ariane said desperately. "And he's searching the Web all the time. If someone takes a photo of you –"

"No one will take a photo," Emily said.

"They might. People take pictures of themselves in here all the time. You just have to show up in the background, like you did in Horseshoe Bay, and –"

"I'll be careful."

"Mom!" Ariane pleaded.

Emily Forsythe shook her head. "No, Ariane. I'm sorry, but I'm not running any more. I can't. I'm staying put. You go do what you need to do, and you'll find me right here when you're done. And then..." She reached out her hand and covered Ariane's with it. "And then we can be together. A family."

Ariane wanted to argue, but she could tell her mom's mind was made up, and what else could she do? Call Wally over in the hopes her mom would pass out again and they could...what? Drag her to the swimming pool and then spirit her away somewhere else? Would that even work? Ariane had a feeling it wouldn't: that the touch of power that remained in her mom, and her rejection of the larger portion of it that Ariane had claimed, would make it impossible for Ariane to use the Lady's power to transport her mother anywhere against her will.

"How's Phyllis?" her mom said then. "I've felt so badly about her, too. But I couldn't tell her I was all right any more than I could tell you."

"She's fine," Ariane said. *She's been held hostage, ensorcelled, and threatened, but she's fine,* she thought – but again, didn't say. Her mom had tried her hardest to take herself out of this whole mess. Anything Ariane said about what had happened so far would only worry her, make her feel guilty, and she could do nothing to help – nothing except do her best to avoid being taken hostage herself. "Will you call her?"

"Oh..." Ariane's mom looked down at the table. "I don't...what would I say? What *could* I say?"

"You'll have to talk to her sooner or later," Ariane said. "I can give her the number where you can reach her. But don't use a cell phone. Do you have a cell phone?"

"No."

"Keep it that way. And don't use any computers."

"Why?"

"Merlin's magic is all through the Internet," Ariane said. "Are you using your real name to work here?"

"Only my first name."

"What last name?"

Emily sighed. "Smith. Not very imaginative, I'm afraid."

"That's good," Ariane said. "Mom, *please* be careful. He really is trying to find you, just like you were afraid he would. And if he finds you...he'll hold you hostage, to force me to give up the shards I have."

"And would you?" her mom said softly.

Ariane nodded fiercely. "Yes," she said. "The sword doesn't mean anything compared to you. I'd give it all up if he had you. So don't let him get you."

"He'll never track me here," her mom said again. "I'm sure of it."

Ariane wasn't, but there didn't seem to be anything else to say about it. She got to her feet. "I'll come back when I can," she said. "When it's safe." Her throat constricted and she had to swallow around a lump. "I don't want to leave," she whispered. "I just found you. But I have to."

"Do what you must, Ariane," her mom said. "We'll be together again soon. I promise."

Ariane nodded. Her mom got to her feet. They hugged, tightly, and again Ariane felt the connection between them, stronger than ever, a connection made of love and magic. She closed her eyes and wished the moment could last forever.

But it couldn't. The shard Wally carried tugged at her, too. And the fourth shard waited to be found – if not by her, then by Major. She released her mom abruptly, and stepped back. "'Bye," she whispered around the renewed lump in her throat, then turned and crossed the Tea Lobby without looking back.

"'Bye," she heard, just barely, as she left her mother behind.

CHAPTER NINE

SWEET AND SALT

WALLY WATCHED ARIANE'S REUNION with her mother from the hallway outside the Tea Lobby, the shard she had pressed into his hand tingling in his pocket. *Tingling?* He glanced down at his jeans. Maybe tingling wasn't the right word. *Vibrating? Thrumming?* Neither seemed quite right, for clearly the shard wasn't vibrating in the usual sense of the word: if he'd pulled it out and held it to his ear, he wouldn't have heard it emitting a pure metallic tone like a tuning fork.

And yet that was the sensation, somehow. Some sense he'd never known he'd had before, the sense that had told him this shard had been hidden on the island in the middle of the lake in New Zealand, and led him right to it, was reacting to the shard's presence, to the magic with which the original Lady of the Lake had imbued the blade centuries ago.

What would it be like, he wondered, to hold the entire sword, whole and reforged? What had Arthur – his distant ancestor, Wally was coming to accept – felt when he'd wielded it? What had his followers seen and reacted to?

Arthur had been an astonishing leader of men, a war

captain beyond compare, winning battle after battle as he united ancient Britain – invincible, it had seemed, while he held Excalibur. Though somehow Mordred had managed to get through the sword's defences. Maybe, Wally thought, because Mordred was Arthur's illegitimate son by his half-sister, Morgause, at least according to some legends. Maybe the fact Mordred shared whatever magical gift his father possessed had interfered with the sword's powers.

Merlin could probably tell me, Wally thought. He snorted. He doubted he'd have the opportunity to ask him – or if he did, it would be only after Merlin captured Wally and held him hostage again.

He stared across the Tea Lobby. Ariane leaped to her feet. He thought she was about to leave. But then her mother got up and hugged her. After a few moments they sat down again.

A man with a blue shirt and a doctor's bag brushed past Wally and headed to the table where the mother and daughter sat. While he talked to Emily, Ariane turned and glanced at Wally. She gave him a thumb's-up. He held up his wrist and tapped his watch, reminding her that every minute spent in Victoria was another minute spent *not* searching for the fourth shard on Cacibajagua Island – and another minute closer to the time when Rex Major arrived on the island and started looking for it himself.

Ariane turned back to her mother. Wally turned and stared down the hall toward the upper lobby. He felt antsy, restless. He could tell some of that feeling – maybe most of it – came from the shard of metal in his pocket. It didn't want to be there. It wanted to get away.

Get away from what? he wondered. Then he looked across the Tea Lobby at Ariane and her mother again. *Or whom?*

The sword clearly didn't like Ariane's mother. He wondered why.

He turned away again abruptly. A little aimless pacing seemed in order. Down to the upper lobby, then back again. Down to the lobby, and back. And again. And again. And...

When Ariane at last emerged from the Tea Lobby, he felt irritated beyond reason at the wait. "Nice of you to finally join me," he snapped. "We do have other places to be, you know." He turned and walked toward the upper lobby once more.

But he'd only made it as far as the entrance to the Empress Dining room before Ariane grabbed his right arm and spun him around. She released him and thrust out her hand. "Give me the shard," she snapped.

Wally glowered at her. The shard thrummed in his pocket. He put his hand in, but didn't take it out. It felt almost alive to his touch. "Maybe I should carry it," he said. "Probably safer with me."

"Wally," Ariane said, her voice low and dangerous. "Give me the shard."

He frowned, and almost rebelled, but then his eyes widened as he realized what was happening. "Crap," he muttered, and jerked the shard out of his pocket and held it out. "Here, take it."

Ariane snatched it from his hand, and immediately his irritation eased. *I've read* The Lord of the Rings, he thought. *You'd think I'd know better.* Excalibur might not be the "One Ring to rule them all," but clearly it shared certain characteristics.

"The shards of Excalibur," he said, "are getting pushy."

Ariane shoved the shard into her backpack, alongside the tensor bandage that normally held it against her side. "I know," she said. "You felt it, too?"

He nodded. "It doesn't like your mom."

"She refused the power of the Lady," Ariane said. "The

sword – or the Lady's power it contains – appears to take that personally." She glanced back into the Tea Lobby. "I can't convince her to run anymore," she said. "She thinks she's safe here. She thinks Rex Major's men can't trace her to the Empress."

Wally shook his head. "I wouldn't bet on it."

"I wouldn't either," Ariane said, sounding almost angry. "But I couldn't change her mind. And it's not like we can take her away by force..." Her voice trailed off. Her eyes widened. She was looking past Wally at someone else. Someone who must be coming toward them.

Crap, he thought. *Crap, crap, crap, crap!*

"Don't turn around," Ariane murmured. "And keep your head down."

"It's Dad, isn't it?" he whispered, looking at his feet.

"Yes," Ariane said. "I recognize him from the pictures in your house."

"Is he alone?"

"He's with another man."

"Which side will they pass us on?"

"Neither. They're stopping."

And now he could hear his father's voice. "Listen, Pete, I know what Sharma said, but the numbers don't add up. I think we need to..." His dad's voice faltered.

"He's looking this way," Ariane whispered. "He's not sure it's you, but he's puzzled. He's going to come over. He's going to say something –"

"He can't know I'm here," Wally said in an agonizing whisper. "If he finds out, Rex Major will know. And if he knows we were here –"

"Mom," Ariane said. "He'll know we were here because of Mom." He didn't dare raise his eyes, but he could tell she had shifted position. "Hang on," she said.

"Why? What –"

He got no farther, because at that moment every fire

sprinkler in the hallway suddenly let go.

As water poured down, and people started screaming and yelling, his father's swearing booming out over everyone else's, Ariane grabbed Wally's hand and ran for the stairs at the corner of the Tea Lobby, past the startled pianist, who was standing up and peering into the hallway to see what was going on. They dashed down the stairs to the lower level and along a long corridor until they found public washrooms. Ariane banged open the door to the women's, called, "Anyone in there?", and when she got no answer, pulled Wally inside.

Five seconds later she'd turned on a tap, stuck her hand into the running water, and spirited them both away.

Wally didn't even know where they were going. He wasn't sure she knew, either. But as it turned out, the journey was very short. They popped up in the same lake in Beacon Hill Park where they'd materialized once before. Since it was now pouring rain, there seemed little reason to climb out on the shore: even standing chest-deep in the lake they were dryer under the bridge – or at least the top parts of them were.

"Where do we go, Wally?" Ariane said. "I can't take us to this Kakki...Cabbi..."

"Cacibajagua," he said helpfully.

"Whatever Island without knowing where it is. I need a map."

"Which means I need a computer," Wally said. He sighed. "Again."

"I don't think going back to the Empress is a good idea," Ariane said.

"Then let's go back to Horseshoe Bay," Wally said. "Even if we're seen by Rex Major's men there it won't tell him anything – he already knows your mom was there, and isn't there now."

"Okay," Ariane said. She took a deep breath. "I wish

I'd had a crumpet or something at the Tea Lobby. I'm starving."

"Me, too."

"I can get us to Horseshoe Bay, but there's no way we get to the Caribbean without something to eat."

"Fish and chips at Troll's," Wally said. "It's a Canadian tradition."

Ariane licked her lips. "That sounds wonderful," she said fervently. "But first things first." She unlimbered her backpack, and rummaged in it, pulling out the shard and the tensor bandage. "Hold this," she said, handing the pack to Wally. Then she pulled her shirt up. Just as her belly button came into view her stomach rumbled, and she made a face.

"Told you I'm starving." She wrapped the bandage around herself again, tucking the blade against her side, then tucked in her shirt once more and shouldered her backpack again. "It's around 1 p.m. here, isn't it?" she said.

Wally nodded.

"Three hours later in Toronto."

He nodded again. "And the same time on Cacibajagua Island."

"By the time we get there, it could be dark."

"Yeah."

"Where will we sleep?"

Wally shook his head. "I don't have a clue," he said. "The place is a resort, but we won't exactly have reservations."

"Guess we'll play it by ear," Ariane said. She gave him a crooked smile. "Seems like that's the only way we ever play it."

"I know," Wally said.

Ariane took his hands, but both of them this time, not just one. Then, before he realized what she intended, she pulled him closer and kissed him, not on the cheek, this time, but on the lips, a soft, lingering kiss that was the sweetest thing he'd ever tasted.

Lips don't really taste sweet, a part of his brain told him. *How could they? They're just skin. A little salty, maybe, or...*

Shut up, another part of his brain suggested. *Just this once, shut up.*

He decided to stop thinking for the duration.

The kiss only lasted a few seconds, but it certainly seemed longer. *Much* longer. He swallowed and opened his eyes, which had closed of their own accord. "Um?" he said – not the wittiest repartee of his life, but it seemed all he could manage. "Um," he repeated for emphasis.

"Thank you, Wally," Ariane whispered. "For helping me find Mom."

"Um!" He cleared his throat. "I mean, thanks. I mean, you're welcome."

Ariane grinned at him, a new kind of a grin, with a hint of shyness in it. He liked it. A lot. "Let's get out of here."

And just like that, Victoria vanished.

◄► ►

Rex Major made it a point to call Wally's and Felicia's parents every day, to reinforce the Commands that kept them from interfering with his plans for their children. He'd already told them of his intention to take Felicia to the Caribbean, but the night before he left he called them again, just to be sure they didn't...worry.

Although, to be honest, Wally and Felicia's mother, at least, hardly seemed to need any reinforcement of the Command not to worry. She was preparing to fly to New Zealand to film a fantasy movie on which she was an assistant director. Major wondered if they'd be shooting near Lake Putahi, where Ariane and Wally had stolen the third shard of Excalibur out from under his nose. "I'm sure Felicia will have a wonderful time," Mrs. Knight said, and that was that.

Mr. Knight didn't even answer his cell phone the first two times Major tried to call him. He got ready for bed, then gave the number one last try. This time Felicia's father answered on the first ring. "Jim Knight here," he said.

"Hi, Jim. It's Rex Major."

"Rex! Wonderful to hear from you." There was no trace of dissembling in Knight's voice. He really *was* thrilled to hear from the one who Commanded him. He had no choice. He would do anything Rex Major asked, without regard for his own dignity, career – or safety.

Major savored the power he held over the other man. He would not abuse that power – but he would use it, if and when it became necessary.

"Just wanted to remind you I'm taking Felicia on a Caribbean weekend adventure tomorrow," he said casually. "You're all right with that." That last phrase was in the Voice of Command, as effective over the telephone as it had once been in person when, as Merlin, he had manipulated all the court of Camelot, excepting Arthur himself.

"I'm all right with that," Knight confirmed cheerfully.

Major resisted the temptation to add, "These are not the droids you're looking for." That particular pop-culture reference had amused him no end once he'd finally seen the scene it referred to: sure, that had been some twenty years after *Star Wars* had first come out – most pop culture didn't interest him, unless you counted opera as pop culture – but better late than never.

"I have wonderful news," Mr. Knight said, unsolicited, much to Merlin's surprise. Mr. Knight rarely initiated a topic of conversation with Major, especially after receiving a Command. "Wally phoned me last night! He's not dead at all. He's back in Canada."

Major, who had been leaning casually back in the chair in his home office, sat up sharply. "He is? Did he say where he was?"

"No," Mr. Knight said. "But he sounded healthy and said he was fine."

"Repeat the conversation to me exactly," Major Commanded, and then listened silently as Knight did so. Wally really had been careful; hadn't given a hint as to where he was calling from. *You'd be surprised how much I move around,* the boy had told his father. Major knew well enough what that meant: thanks to Ariane's power, he could have been calling from anywhere in Canada – anywhere in the world, come to that.

But while the conversation didn't give him any clues as to where Wally and Ariane could be found right now, it did tell him where they were likely to be very soon.

Wally Knight's father had told Wally that Rex Major and Felicia were heading to the Caribbean. Almost certainly, Wally and Ariane would magic their way down there in the hope of beating him to the shard once more.

But it won't do them any good, Rex Major thought. *The Caribbean is a big place, with hundreds of islands. And I'm taking my private jet to a private island. There's no way they can know which island. And with the shard under salt water, as I believe it to be, Ariane will no more be able to sense its location from down there than she can from up here, at least not until I retrieve it – at which point it will be too late.*

Then he frowned, because he would have wagered that Wally could not possibly have figured out where he was going in New Zealand, either, yet somehow the boy had. He'd assumed that was because Wally had had access to his private emails at the time, not to mention his banking information. Clearly the boy had siphoned several thousand dollars out of an account he paid little attention to, which was why it had taken him so long to notice. The little brat did have a way of surprising him. And Ariane too, thanks to the power poured into her by Merlin's once-beloved sister, the Lady of the Lake, kept surprising him in unpleasant ways.

Just because he couldn't *see* any way for them to trace him to Cacibajagua Island didn't mean they *couldn't*. He'd have to be ready for that eventuality.

"Anything else interesting happen?" he said, more by rote than because he expected a useful response; but once again Mr. Knight surprised him.

"Something very strange in the hotel this morning," Knight said. "I was talking to Peter Farmington from the local office outside the Empress Dining Room, and all of a sudden all of the water sprinklers in that hallway let go at once. We were soaked to the skin. They shut them off pretty quick, but it caused quite a lot of damage, as you can imagine."

Major snapped alert again. "Describe exactly what you saw, starting just before that happened," he Commanded, and Knight obliged – which was how Rex Major found out that a young boy with red hair and an older girl with black hair had been in the hallway just before the sprinkler let go; how the boy had reminded Mr. Knight of his son; how, during the confusion, the two had vanished.

Major thanked Knight and wished him good night without really hearing his own voice. His mind was in overdrive, putting two and two together and getting a very pleasing four.

Wally Knight and Ariane Forsythe had been at the Fairmont Empress, at the very moment his men were on the ferry from Horseshoe Bay to Nanaimo, following the trail of Emily Forsythe, the one person whom, after Wally and Ariane themselves, Major most wanted to find.

Could they have been there because Wally wanted to

contact his father? Major discounted that possibility immediately – as soon as Jim Knight had seen his son, Ariane had created a diversion and they had disappeared. Their presence at the Empress *could* have been a coincidence – but it seemed an awfully big one.

Wally was very good with computers – Major knew that well enough – and if his own computer people had been able to identify Emily Forsythe in photos taken at Horseshoe Bay, quite likely Wally had been, too. He and Ariane could be following the same trail as Major's men, but they might well have information he lacked. Rather than go to Nanaimo, where Ariane's mother had gone on the ferry just a couple of weeks ago, perhaps they had gone straight to her ultimate destination: Victoria. Not only Victoria, but the Fairmont Empress.

It was extremely doubtful Emily Forsythe had the funds to stay at the grand old hotel. Which meant she was most likely working there, or had been.

Had Wally and Ariane found her? He couldn't be certain of that, but they'd clearly thought that was the place to look. Which meant that was where his men should be looking, not in Nanaimo.

He opened his laptop and sent a quick email. Then he used the thread of magic that ran through the Web to find Jim Knight's cell phone account. He checked the incoming-calls log and saw that the man had received two calls the previous evening. He used the service provider's reverse-look-up function. One of the calls was from a real estate development company in Victoria: probably some client working late and needing a piece of information from the management consultant.

The second caller had hidden his or her number from Call Display. But that didn't matter to Major: the phone number had still been sent, and it displayed for *him*. The call had come from the Medicine Hat Lodge, from a room rented by someone called Emma Macphail. A quick Google search revealed a retired Saskatchewan schoolteacher by that name, currently residing in Estevan.

There was no obvious connection to Wally or Ariane. Perhaps they had somehow gained access to her room to use the phone? But he checked one more suspicion and found that, yes, indeed, the Medicine Hat Lodge had a swimming pool: the perfect place for Ariane to begin and end one of her trips.

He thought for a moment, then created another watching function for his magical outreach into the Internet: any record anywhere of Wally Knight or Ariane Forsythe in Medicine Hat would send him an immediate email alert. After a moment he made an addition – from now on he'd also keep an eye on this Emma Macphail.

Satisfied, he closed the computer, got up, and got ready for bed.

Tomorrow promised to be an interesting day in very many ways.

CHAPTER TEN

CARIBBEAN NIGHT

ARIANE SAT WITH WALLY in Troll's Restaurant in Horse-shoe Bay. Plates that had been piled with battered fish and french fries now bore nothing but a few smears of catsup and tartar sauce. They'd already materialized in Whyte Lake as before, then made their way down to the Horse-shoe Bay Motel and used the computer; the desk clerk, remembering Wally from earlier in the day, had just waved at them as they passed. They had printed out a map show-ing the location of Cacibajagua Island and Wally had looked up the weather they could expect. Though there was no forecast for Cacibajagua itself, he'd easily found one for the relatively nearby Turks and Caicos. "Weird," he said to Ariane, turning toward her. "There's a storm forming, even though hurricane season is over. Usually they only get a few evening thunderstorms in December. But this is a big one – the sky is already overcast over hun-dreds of square kilometres, and they're expecting heavy rain and wind within thirty-six hours. High of 82 Fahren-heit for tomorrow."

"What is that in Celsius?"

Wally grinned. "Around 28."

She smiled back. "Well, at least we won't be materializing in freezing water for once. And overcast skies – that's good, isn't it?"

"I guess. But if it storms..." Wally bent back over the computer. While he studied the satellite images on the screen, she studied him. She'd only known him for two months. He still looked young for his age, but along with the few centimetres he'd gained since they'd met had come quite a few more muscles, too.

And she'd kissed him.

She still couldn't believe she'd done that. It had just kind of...happened. It had seemed like the right thing to do. And it had been...nice.

More than nice. Quite wonderful, actually.

He'd looked up at her suddenly, and she'd glanced away, hoping he hadn't seen her blushing – or maybe hoping he had.

That wasn't the only wonderful thing that had happened today. The connection she had felt with her mother, the connection built on the Lady's blood they both shared, hadn't vanished when they'd returned to Horseshoe Bay. She could still feel it – and that meant she'd never lose her mother again. It had given an added glow to the past few hours and an added relish to the food, which she'd devoured. She'd been using a lot of power and not replenishing it, so the fish and chips and a generous helping of apple crisp with ice cream had vanished in remarkably short order – short enough order that even Wally, the human vacuum cleaner, had remarked on it.

Now, as darkness gathered on the water across the street and park from where they sat, they had to plan their next move.

"I think we go now," Ariane said.

"It'll be the middle of the night when we arrive," Wally pointed out. "And we don't know what we'll find.

We might not even be able to find enough fresh water to materialize in."

"Better to find that out tonight than in the morning when Rex Major is already on his way," Ariane argued. "If we end up having to go to the Turks and Caicos to find a pool, then get a boat to take us to the island at first light, we'll need every minute we can spare." Until she'd said that out loud, she hadn't realized that that might actually be what they'd have to do. She frowned. "How much money do we have?"

Wally looked around to make sure nobody could overhear him then leaned in close. "We've got about $2,000 in cash with us," he whispered. "Hidden in the lining of my backpack."

Ariane's eyes widened. "That much?"

Wally nodded. "I've been carrying it everywhere I go," he said. "Just in case."

"Then that's the plan," Ariane said. "We go straight to the island if we can. If we can't, we get as close as we can and hire a boat in the morning."

She hushed as she saw the waitress approaching, the same one they'd talked to earlier in the day. "Can I get you kids anything else?" she said.

"No, we're good," Wally said.

"Here's the bill, then," the waitress said. "No rush." She gave them a smile – a rather knowing smile, Ariane thought – and went to greet a family of four that had just come in the door.

"She thinks we're on a date," Wally said. He'd clearly seen the waitress's expression, too. He gave Ariane a shy grin.

"Little does she know we're actually plotting to save the world from an evil sorcerer," Ariane said. But she felt her own mouth curve into a smile. "I'd rather we were just having dinner before going to a movie."

"Me, too," Wally said.

"Some day," Ariane said.

That produced an awkward silence. Ariane drank the last of her Diet Coke to cover it, then got to her feet. "Let's get going."

They took the bill to the front and Wally paid cash; then they went out into the dark, dank, drizzling night, crossing the street to the park to be away from prying eyes. Ariane held out her hand and Wally took it, his fingers warm in hers. She exerted a little of her power, drying them and pushing the raindrops away, so that they stood perfectly dry even as water pattered all around.

"Ready?" she said.

"Ready."

She squeezed his hand, and together they leaped into the clouds.

Ariane felt both immensely large and frighteningly immaterial, like a giant shadow puppet cast on the clouds by some powerful light. As always, she felt the urge to let herself expand even farther, to join with the clouds and leave her consciousness behind forever, but she suppressed it, helped by the bright hard core of the shard of Excalibur she carried, the piece of steel that would never allow itself to be destroyed in that way. She was also helped by the sense of Wally's presence, mingled with hers within the clouds in an intimate fashion that would be intensely embarrassing to think about too much, so she tried not to. Instead, she focussed her attention on the journey ahead.

Every time she used her power this way it became easier to navigate, to correlate the clouds and the land below with the features of the map she had consulted. They rushed away through the billows of vapour, not in anything like a straight line, following weather fronts to keep to the clouds, making short leaps across empty air in some places, dropping down into streams and lakes in others, the kilometres flashing by faster than the fastest jet. As always, Ariane had no sense of time passing, so she couldn't be certain how long it took them to cross the continent diagonally from northwest to southeast, but it was still only the middle of the night when they flashed out over the Atlantic. She felt the salt water below, a different feeling than the land over which they had been passing: she could no more make use of earth than she could of salt water, but the earth was neutral, whereas the sea felt coldly inimical, mocking her power, all that water forever beyond her control.

The clouds were fresh water, though, and it was through the clouds they flashed, until the strange near-sight sense the Lady's power gave her showed her Caciba-jagua Island below despite the darkness all around. Shaped rather like a comma, with a round, fat part on the south end tapering to a long, curving tail at the north, it was no more than ten kilometres long and maybe half as wide where it was fattest. A small hotel crouched on the eastern side of the broader part of the island, between an inland airstrip and a long, wooden dock where several boats bobbed at anchor.

Most important, though, the Lady's power showed her the small freshwater lake near the centre of the hilly interior. There was also a swimming pool at the hotel, but there'd be no way to materialize there without being seen, and so she took them down into the lake.

One moment they were amorphous mingled blobs of magical something-or-other in the clouds, the next they were solid Ariane and Wally. They spluttered to the surface and stood in shoulder-deep, milk-warm water.

Surrounded by hills that blocked all light from the resort, and with the sky overcast, the lake was pitch-black. Ariane knew Wally was close at hand, because she could hear him breathing, but she couldn't see a thing.

More wonderful, she discovered she could still sense

her mother, back in Victoria. The sensation made her smile in the darkness.

"Too bad we don't need to develop film," Wally's disembodied voice said.

Ariane laughed. "I can tell where the shore is," she said. "I can feel everything in the water...including you." She reached out a hand toward him.

"Ow!" he said. "That's my nose."

"Sorry," Ariane said.

His fingers found hers and she squeezed them as she had before they'd begun the journey. "This way," she said, and led him toward what her Lady-of-the-Lake-powered senses told her was the nearest shore, just a few metres away. They clambered out onto big, rounded rocks, in air that felt as warm and almost as wet as the water had, and sat down while Ariane ordered them dry – although in this weather, they'd soon be sweating. She took off the coat she'd been wearing in Horseshoe Bay and stuffed it into her backpack. She could hear Wally presumably doing the same, then rummaging in his backpack some more; moments later a flashlight came on. "That's better," he said, and flashed the light around.

Dark water, green trees, black rocks.

"Not very informative," Ariane said.

"Not the kind of terrain you want to stumble around in, in the dark," Wally agreed.

And dark though it was, it was far from quiet. Sound filled the night: creakings and croakings and chirpings and warblings.

"They don't have any big predators on Caribbean islands," Wally said after a moment. "I'm sure I read that somewhere."

Something squawked so loud Ariane's heart jumped to double time. "I hope you're right," she said. Another squawk, or maybe a shriek, came from her right, followed by a splash. Something had just jumped into the lake. Wally flashed his light in that direction, but all Ariane saw was spreading ripples. "Maybe this wasn't such a good idea," she said nervously.

"That depends," Wally said. "Can you sense the shard?"

Ariane closed her eyes and concentrated. The shard she carried with her sang its song as always at her side, and she could even sense the first shard, tucked away back in Saskatchewan, just as she could sense her mother in Victoria. The shard Merlin carried was hidden from her while it was in his possession. And the fourth, the one they thought was somewhere on this island...

Nothing.

Ariane opened her eyes – not that it made much difference – and said, "No."

Wally turned and aimed his light away from the lake, into the surrounding jungle. The circle of illumination slid over what looked like an impenetrable tangle of vines and undergrowth. "We can't hike through that," Ariane said. "And we can't just sit here all night. Maybe we should go to the Turks and Caicos, get a boat in the morning, or else come back when it's light –"

"Wait a second," Wally said. "I just glimpsed –"

He was twisted around on the rock where he sat. Now he aimed the light to Ariane's left. She turned her head and saw what he had spotted: a signpost, shaped to look as though it had been roughly carved from driftwood, though it looked a little too *perfectly* roughly carved, if that made sense, like a prop from Disneyland's Jungle Cruise. "Welcome to Lake Tanama (Butterfly Lake)," Wally read out loud. "No swimming."

"Oops," Ariane said, glancing uneasily at the water they'd just clambered out of. "I wonder why?"

"Some sort of parasite, maybe," Wally said absently.

"Could be *Schistosoma* worms."

"Shkisto-*what?*" Ariane almost shrieked.

"But probably not!" Wally said hastily. "Wouldn't you be able to sense them?"

"How do I know?" She stretched her awareness throughout the warm water. She had no idea what a *Schistosoma* worm even was, but all she sensed were small fish and... "Yuck!"

"What?" Wally said.

"Leeches. Down in the mud." She shuddered and withdrew her awareness from the water. "No wading if we can help it."

Wally shone the light on his own face, gave her a quick grin that was probably supposed to be reassuring but of course looked like a Halloween mask with the light under his chin, and then swung the light back to the signpost. "There's more," he said, moving the light lower. "Look."

"The Resort," she read on one carefully shaped and mounted piece of "driftwood." The pointy end of it indicated a path into the forest. "The Jujo Cataract," read the other sign. It pointed along the shore of the lake, where she now saw there was a boardwalk. They weren't in uncharted wilderness after all. "What's a Jujo?"

"That's the name of the underwater cave that's the whole reason for this resort," Wally said excitedly. "And the Jujo Cataract has to be the freshwater waterfall that pours into it at this end. That path will take us straight to the shard!"

"If it's there," Ariane said, trying to temper the sudden leap of hope and excitement in her heart. But she was already getting to her feet. "Let's go!"

The sounds of the warm, humid night suddenly seemed nothing more than the soundtrack of a Caribbean-vacation TV commercial as they stepped onto the boardwalk. *Amazing what a touch of civilization can do,* Ariane thought.

The boardwalk led along the shore of the lake, threading its way between rocks and jungle on one side and black water on the other. After a few hundred metres Ariane began to hear a new sound in the noisy night: the rush of water.

"You hear that?" she said.

Wally nodded. They hurried forward.

The boardwalk ended abruptly, becoming a square platform surrounded on three sides by a railing. To their right, the lake also ended, water pouring from it through a rocky gap and falling away in white spray into darkness beyond. "Dead end," Wally said, sounding disappointed. "The water must tumble all the way down the hill before it drops into the cave."

Ariane laughed at him. She felt almost giddy with hope. "Dead end?" she said. "Aren't you forgetting something?"

He looked at her, face puzzled in the dim light the railing reflected back from the flashlight beam.

"I'm the freaking Lady of the Lake," she said. She got down on her hands and knees. "Put the flashlight away and take hold."

Wally laughed. "Right." The light went out. She heard his backpack zip. She felt his hand around her ankle. She reached out and stuck her hand into the smooth curve of water falling into darkness, and then she and Wally fell with it.

CHAPTER ELEVEN

THE CAVE AND THE CATARACT

WALLY BARELY HAD TIME TO REMEMBER how much he hated being dissolved into water before, with horrifying, shocking suddenness, he was back in his body, and floundering: not in fresh water, but salt. He choked, his clothes and backpack pulling him down. He still had hold of Ariane's ankle: he held to it like the drowning man he was about to become. The water fell away from him and he gasped air. "Ariane!" he gasped. "What...?"

"It's okay!" she shouted. "There's a ladder!"

"But I can't –"

See, he wanted to say, but the water, clearly connected to the sea somewhere, had surged upward again, plunging him under. He gripped Ariane's ankle even more tightly. "...got to let go of me!" he heard her shouting at him as his head broke the surface again.

"No!"

"It's all right! My foot's on the rung – just let go and grab the ladder instead."

Another surge of seawater, lifting him up so that his head banged into Ariane's leg. As the water fell away this time he released her ankle and lunged with both hands, scrabbling in the dark. He felt the wooden rung of a ladder under his right hand, gripped it, found it with his left as well. When the sea rose again, he held on to the ladder instead of Ariane, who he sensed had climbed above him. Gulping air, he followed.

They clambered out onto another wooden platform.

"I'm an idiot," Ariane gasped in the dark. "I thought...I don't know what I thought. Salt water." She shuddered. "I hate it. It feels...dirty to me. It hates me."

"It hates the Lady," Wally said. "Can you at least dry us?"

"I think so," Ariane said. And suddenly he felt the water fly off his body, almost as weird a sensation, despite how often he'd experienced it, as being dissolved into stream or cloud. He still felt uncomfortable, though, as though his skin were crusted.

"Let me guess," he said. "The water went away, but the minerals stayed behind."

"Feels like it," Ariane said. "I didn't notice that when we hit Hudson's Bay on that test trip...remember?"

"I remember," Wally said. "But then, at the time we were mostly focussed on not freezing to death. At least there's no danger of *that.*"

"Does the flashlight still work?"

"It's waterproof. It'd better." Wally dug in his backpack, found the flashlight, turned it on. He swept it around.

They stood on a dock, currently quite high above the surging seawater, no doubt designed to still clear the surface at high tide. He leaned over the edge and flashed the light down. From the looks of the posts supporting the dock, the tide was either halfway in or halfway out at the moment. He turned the light toward the sound of rushing water. The Jujo Cataract, their highway down the hillside, fell through a black hole in the cave's ceiling.

Presumably the whole chamber was a lot better lit when divers came calling.

That gave him an idea. He shone the light around some more, and quickly spotted what he'd suspected might be there: lights all around the cavern, waterproof and tucked away in odd corners of the stone walls and roof. But though he looked, he could see no switch to turn the lights on.

It wouldn't be down here where the water reaches, he reasoned. *It must be...*

He lifted the light.

A wooden stairway led up about ten metres, into the night air. His light barely extended that far, but he glimpsed some kind of structure at the top. More clearly, he saw electrical cables, strung on the underside of the stairs' handrail. "Up there," he said to Ariane, gesturing with the flashlight.

She squinted up the stairs. "What is it?"

"Some kind of hut," he said. "I'm betting there's a switch inside to turn on the lights down here. If it works, we might be able to see what we're doing...maybe well enough to find the shard."

"But can we get into it?" she said doubtfully. "Won't it be locked?"

"On a private island? Why would it be?" Wally started up the stairs. "Only one way to find out."

The hut continued the *faux*-castaway style of the signposts. It appeared to be made of roughly cobbled-together wood, roofed with palm fronds, but a closer look revealed sturdy square-cut timber in the walls and a tin roof beneath the palms. The electrical cables entered through an opening in the foundation.

As Wally had hoped, only a latch secured the wooden door, not a lock. He pulled the door open and flashed the light around the interior.

The building was about four metres on a side, with a

small window in every wall. Under the window across from the door, a simple wooden bench stretched the hut's length. A blue metal toolbox rested on one corner of the bench, alongside a large first-aid kit. Along the wall to the left hung rope, several orange life preservers, flippers, and snorkels. And to the right...

"Ah," Wally said in satisfaction. He went over the red-painted junction box and flipped the big switch on its side.

Light stabbed his eyes. "Ow," he said, at the same moment as Ariane.

"Warn me next time!" she complained, squinting at him.

"Sorry," he said. He turned off the flashlight and returned it to his backpack. "Now let's go see what's what."

They went back out onto the staircase and down into the cave.

It had been transformed. Carefully placed spotlights had turned the cataract into a glittering ribbon of diamonds. The seawater – higher than it had been, Wally saw, which meant the tide was coming in, not going out – now glowed a beautiful blue-green, lit from below. Other lights cast dramatic shadows over the rugged walls, which sparkled with both moisture and growths of crystals.

"It's beautiful," Ariane whispered.

Wally agreed, but they weren't there to sightsee. "You still can't feel the shard?

Ariane shook her head. "No," she said. "If it's here, it's still under salt water."

Wally stared down into the pool. Seawater continued to surge and recede. He could feel the change in pressure each time in his chest and ears, as though the vast space were breathing – as though it were alive.

"If the Lady hid the shard here," he said, "She would have had to have put it somewhere near the cataract...wouldn't she? She couldn't have entered the seawater."

"I don't know," Ariane said. "I don't know what the Lady could or couldn't do. I have her power, but she wasn't even human. She was from Faerie. She might have been able to do things I'll never be able to do. It's not like she gave me an operating manual. Merlin drove her out of the world before she could do much of anything, remember?"

Since Wally knew that Merlin had found the Lady because he'd carried his smartphone into her presence when he'd followed Ariane down the mystical watery staircase into Wascana Lake, he remembered all too well.

"We need to search down in the water," he said.

"I don't know how to scuba dive," Ariane said.

"Neither do I," Wally said. "But we can both swim. Even me." He knew he wasn't a great swimmer, even yet, but the strange boost in strength and endurance and physical skill he'd noted while fencing, that he now knew came from the awakening shards of Excalibur, had carried over to other things, too. He'd managed to swim out to the island in the middle of Lake Putahi when they'd been after the third shard. He could manage swimming in this pool of salt water. It wasn't nearly as big as the lake had been. "Up in the hut," he indicated the stairs, "are snorkels and diving masks. And we've both got our swimsuits in our backpacks, so we won't have to skinny-dip." *Unfortunately*, he thought about adding as a joke, but quickly decided against.

"It's worth a..." Ariane's reply was swallowed midway by an enormous yawn. She bit it off and finished, "...try." She rubbed her eyes. "Sorry, Wally," she said. "I'm wearing out. I need sleep. If we can't find it right away, we'll have to wait until daylight and give me a chance to recharge." She turned and started back up the stairs.

Wally followed her, but waited outside the hut while she changed into her swimsuit. Then it was his turn. He stripped out of his clothes and tugged on his trunks, then stuffed his salt-stained T-shirt and jeans, underwear, socks and running shoes into the pack. He took the waterproof flashlight, pushing his wrist through the cord that dangled from its end and tightening it so it wouldn't slip off, but left his backpack on the workbench next to Ariane's. Then he grabbed two masks and two snorkels and went out again, the humid air warm against his bare skin. *Swimsuits make more sense than clothes in this climate,* he thought. Although if the sun came out in the morning he'd want to cover up quick or his torso would quickly become the same colour as his hair.

Together he and Ariane padded down the stairs again. He checked his waterproof watch, and did the mental calculations. "It's just shy of 10 p.m. here," he said as they descended. "Late enough we shouldn't be surprised by anyone." Assuming it had taken them most of an hour to get to this point from their arrival in the lake, that meant they had made the journey from Horseshoe Bay to the Caribbean in about two hours. *Pretty impressive,* he thought. *I wonder how fast Ariane could make the trip if she knew* exactly *where she was going?* He glanced up at the sky. It remained blank and black. "With a storm headed this way, maybe the island will be socked in in the morning and Rex Major won't be able to fly here."

"Wishful thinking," Ariane said, and Wally knew she was right: the storm was still a day and a half away, according to the forecast.

Down on the platform, he handed her a mask and snorkel and a set of fins, and took the others for himself. The water continued to rise. They'd had to climb up six rungs on the ladder when they'd materialized. Now only four were showing, and the sound of the cataract falling into the seawater had changed.

"How far does the water fall at low tide?" Ariane said,

sitting on the platform as she pulled the flippers onto her bare feet, her mask pushed up on her forehead. There was an odd bulge around the middle of her sleek black one-piece swimsuit; the shard of Excalibur strapped to her side.

"I don't know," Wally said as he tugged on his own fins. "Tides are pretty minimal in the Caribbean, but this is a long, skinny cave that's probably much wider at the other end than it is at this one. So even if it only rises and falls a metre at that end, it could rise and fall a lot more at this end. Sort of like what happens in the Bay of Fundy."

Ariane shot him a look. "How do you know all this stuff, anyway?"

"I read," Wally said uncomfortably. He knew he could come across as a know-it-all. Flish had always hated it.

And now Flish hates me.

Once he and his sister had been not just family but friends. But that was before his family had shattered into broken shards like those of the sword Excalibur – and the edges of those shards were just as sharp and cutting, though he felt the pain in his heart instead of his flesh. He raised a hand to the fading scar on his cheek, left by the second shard of the sword when Ariane had called it to her in the cave in France.

That cave had almost proved disastrous, to the quest and to their friendship.

He hoped they'd have better luck in this one.

"Let's see what we can see," he said. He got to his feet, flapped awkwardly in his fins to the edge of the platform, pulled the mask down, adjusted the snorkel, and started down the ladder.

A moment later they were both in the water, staring down through the masks at the bottom of the cave beneath the sea.

Unrealistically, Wally had hoped maybe they'd see some sort of treasure chest, just the right size to contain the fourth shard of the sword. But of course if anything had been in plain sight it would have been picked up long before. The cave was visited not only by divers almost every day, but by a freaking submarine! It wasn't a very *big* submarine – it only held five people, from what Wally had read on the resort website – but still.

Instead, all he saw was rough stone, with here and there a large, loose boulder resting on it.

Wait a minute, he thought. *Loose boulders?*

He turned and swam as close to the cataract as he dared – not too close, because the closer he got to the wall the more the rise and fall of the water threatened to throw him against the rocks. He looked right and saw Ariane floating nearby. He turned his attention back to the bottom of the cave. At the base of the cataract lay a pile of loose rock, which had clearly fallen from somewhere up above.

The Caribbean has earthquakes, he thought. *And the shard was placed here a thousand years ago. If the Lady hid it in the cave at the base of the cataract, and then there was an earthquake...*

He stared at the rocks a few moments longer, breathing steadily through the snorkel, remembering another lake, on the other side of the world, high up in the mountains of New Zealand. When he'd reached *that* lake, he'd somehow known that the third shard was on the small island near its centre. He had his own connection to Excalibur, and it had nothing to do with the power of the Lady of the Lake. And that meant that maybe, just maybe, his power wasn't negated by salt water.

He couldn't sense anything yet. But if he got closer...

He took a deep breath through the snorkel, and dove. The fins helped as he angled his hands to drive himself as deep as he could. But the water continued to surge, and in among the rocks at the bottom of the cataract, it also swirled. It seemed to seize him like a giant hand. He lost control.

It twirled him around and drove him against the rocks.

He curled up just in time, hands over his heads. His shoulder banged painfully against rough stone, and his held breath whooshed out in a torrent of bubbles. Then the water receded, tugging him away from the stone, and he straightened and drove, chest bursting, up toward the surface.

He spat out the snorkel mouthpiece and sucked air, mixed with just enough salt water that he choked. Then Ariane had hold of him, pulling him with her, back toward the dock. They crawled out onto the wooden platform together, and, still on his hands and knees, he coughed and spat, trying to get his breath.

"Are you crazy?" Ariane shouted. She took hold of his shoulders, pulled him back until he sat on his haunches. "You could have been killed!"

"Didn't...expect...the current," Wally gasped out. He took a deep breath, the first one he hadn't choked on.

"What were you trying to do? There's nothing down there...nothing but rocks. The shard's not here." He could hear the bitter disappointment in her voice.

"Yes, it is," he said. He swiped the back of his arm across his mouth, then twisted around to look at the tumbled rocks at the base of the cataract, where the falling water dashed into white spray before pouring in a thousand separate streams down into the seawater. "It's buried beneath those rocks, somewhere at the very bottom, where it's always under salt water."

"You don't know that," Ariane snapped. "You're just guessing."

"I do know it." Wally touched his shoulder. "Ow."

"You're bleeding," Ariane said, her voice softening with concern. "Wally –"

"It's nothing," he said impatiently. "Ariane, I'm telling you the shard is there."

"But how can you –"

"I felt it," he said. "I sensed it. It's there. And when Merlin gets into this cave, he's going to sense it, too." He looked down at the rocks: tonnes and tonnes of tumbled rocks, brought down by a shrug of the Earth's crust some time in the past millennium. He touched his aching shoulder, and stared at the redness covering his fingers. "It's there," he repeated dully. He felt a little dazed. "But I don't see any way for us to get to it."

"There's a first-aid kit in the hut," Ariane said. "Let's get you up there."

◄◄ ►►

Ariane followed Wally up the stairs, feeling sick to her stomach as she looked at the blood running down his bare back from the cut in his shoulder. It wasn't the blood that made her feel ill – she'd never been queasy at the sight of blood – but the fact that Wally had gotten hurt trying to help her fulfill her quest. *Everyone I love is in danger all the time because of me,* she thought bitterly. *Because I agreed to accept the Lady's power. Because I was selfish. "What have you done?" Mom asked. And she was right. What have I done?*

It hadn't felt like the selfish thing to do at the time. It had felt like the *selfless* thing to do. Like the heroine of a fantasy novel, she would give up being an ordinary girl so she could stop the evil Merlin from taking over the world.

But had that ever been the real reason? Or had she really just wanted power, power to make the bullies stop bullying, power to finally take control of her own life after being out of control for so long, shunted from home to home and school to school before finally landing with Aunt Phyllis?

I should just give up, give Merlin the shards I have, let him win. It would be better for everyone.

But she knew that wasn't true. He would make the world an armed camp from which to attack Faerie. Besides, the shards of Excalibur wouldn't let her. The power she had accepted from the Lady wouldn't let her. She had to complete the quest. She had to *win*.

Which meant she needed this fourth shard. Then she would have three. With three, she would surely find the hilt, the final piece; and she had been told that when she had that much of the sword, Merlin could not stop her from taking the final piece from him.

Wally said he could sense the shard in the pile of fallen rock at the base of the cataract. She had no choice but to believe him. He was convinced he was the heir of Arthur, just as she was the heir of the Lady of the Lake, and the fact Merlin had decided Wally's sister, Flish, would serve just as well as Wally himself spoke to the truth of that belief. So did the way the sword reacted to Wally. Only when he held two shards did they sing in harmony as they were meant to. And he had found the third shard on the island in New Zealand before she had.

But knowing the shard was at the base of the cataract brought them no closer to reaching it, not when it was buried under tonnes of rock – not when that rock, in turn, was submerged in seawater. She could do nothing with that horrible stuff. Just swimming in it had made her skin crawl.

I'm tired, drained. But we'll figure it out, she promised herself. *We will. We have to. Because Merlin will be here in a few hours, and if we don't, he will.*

They'd reached the top of the stairs. Ariane opened the

door to the hut and Wally went in and sat down on the stool tucked next to the workbench. Ariane grabbed the first-aid kit from its place beside the toolbox, pulled it open, and took out a package of gauze pads. She removed one from its wrapping and put it on the wound, a shallow cut maybe seven centimetres long.

"Do you know first aid?" Wally said.

"Believe it or not, I do," Ariane said. "I took a course at my last school, the one before Oscana. I thought it might come in handy if I got beat up."

"Oh," Wally said.

A silence.

Then he asked, "Will it need stitches?"

"Can't be sure yet," Ariane said, "but I don't think so. It's shallow and not gaping. I'm supposed to hold this in place for ten minutes. That should stop the bleeding. But if it doesn't...we'll have to go to the resort."

Wally jerked. "No," he said. "Merlin will find us."

"Better that than you bleeding to death or being scarred for life," Ariane said sharply. "Quit moving."

Wally subsided.

They were both dripping wet. Ariane realized she could do something about that, and ordered them dry. Of course, that just left them covered with a thin crust of minerals. She sighed. "I hate salt water."

"How do we get to the shard?" Wally said.

"I don't know," Ariane said. "It would take dynamite. And I don't think there's any of that in this hut. Now hold still. I'm going to pull the gauze away." She suited actions to words. She put the red-stained pad on the workbench and studied the wound. No fresh blood welled from it. "It's stopped bleeding." She reached for the kit, took out an antibacterial cream, and smeared it liberally on a new gauze pad. She placed that on the wound then taped it in place. "Does it hurt?"

"Yeah," Wally said. He sounded a little shaky. "It hurts."

Ariane rummaged in the first-aid kit and found a bottle of ibuprofen. She shook out two tablets and handed them to him, along with a bottle of water from her backpack. He took them gratefully and downed them. "Try not to move your shoulder too much or you'll start it bleeding again," she said as she returned the bottle of pills to the kit.

"That could be difficult," Wally said. "If we're going after the shard."

"We're not going after the shard," Ariane said. She suddenly felt as heavy as lead, as though every ounce of her energy had fled her body at once. Her mind felt dull, unable to deal with any more problems. "We can't get to it. We just can't."

"Ariane –"

"We *can't*, Wally." She sat down on the floor, her back to the closed door. "We're going to have to wait for Major to show up. We'll see what he does. Maybe he'll uncover the shard for us, and we can go after it then. But there's no way we can get it ourselves, Wally. Not while it's under seawater." She closed her eyes. "And I have no strength left," she whispered. "None at all."

She only intended to rest her eyes for a minute. But it had been a long and difficult day, and she'd been using her power heavily.

Before she was even aware of it, she was asleep.

◄ ►

Wally sat on the stool and looked down at the sleeping Ariane. She had slid softly, bonelessly, onto her side. She looked soft and vulnerable, exposed, lying there in her swimsuit, eyes closed. His heart ached with the need to help her, to protect her. He swallowed.

But she was right. There was nothing they could do. Nothing they could do to break those rocks. Even if they had been submerged in fresh water, not salt, he doubted she could do anything with them. They were too big. Water would just flow around them. Like she'd said, they needed explosives, or some other way to force the rocks apart.

He got up and turned off the master switch that had activated the lights in the cavern and in the hut. In the sudden, complete darkness, he lay down on the floor next to Ariane. His shoulder ached from being slammed against the rocks. He was lucky he hadn't broken anything. The cut was a sharper-edged, fiery pain within the dull throb of the bruise, but it seemed to be hurting a little less – probably the painkillers taking hold.

Between the pain and the hard wooden floor he'd never be able to sleep. He'd just lie there and rest until first light. Then they'd have to get out of the hut before they were discovered.

He closed his eyes, his mind still on the problem of the rocks. His thoughts drifted back through everything he had seen Ariane do. The memories became jumbled. The diamond mine in the Northwest Territories...the cave in southern France...the lake in the clouds...the "explosion" in the tennis courts behind the school...facing Flish and her "coven" in the hallway...

...tendrils of water, hardening to ice, smashing holes in the lockers...

His eyes jerked open. "Ice," he breathed. "Ice!"

Ariane could turn water to ice. And ice –

Ice expanded.

Ice destroyed.

Ice broke rocks.

Ice!

He sat up, wincing as his shoulder reacted, reached out

with his hand to shake Ariane awake...and then stopped. He could hear her slow, steady breathing. He remembered how she had looked, lying there, exhausted, how he had wanted to protect her.

Morning is soon enough, he thought. *Morning won't make any difference. She'll need all the power she can muster. And that means she needs sleep.*

And food. He frowned. The fish and chips in Horseshoe Bay seemed ages ago, though it was only a few hours. And they would run out of water soon enough as well. They'd only brought a couple of bottles apiece. Sure, the waterfall was fresh water, but remembering the "No Swimming" sign up above, not to mention the leeches, he didn't think drinking from it would be the wisest course of action.

Time enough to worry about it in the morning. Even if Rex Major left Toronto at dawn, he wouldn't get to the island until late morning. They still had time to beat him, to take the shard before he could get to it.

He lay back down again, resolving to stay awake until dawn, then rouse Ariane.

He woke to full daylight in the hut and the sound of the door opening.

"What the *hell?*" boomed a voice.

CHAPTER TWELVE

CASTAWAYS

UNWILLING TO WASTE ANY TIME, Rex Major had asked for his private jet to be ready to depart at 7 a.m. That meant getting up before 5 a.m., of course, but that was a small hardship for him. Arthur had not been one to let his army lie abed: when the King had said his men would move or attack at first light, he'd meant it. And though Merlin had not accompanied Arthur on all his military campaigns, he had been on enough of them to have learned the old soldier's trick of both falling asleep and coming awake and alert at a moment's notice.

Felicia Knight, on the other hand...

He started by knocking on the girl's door. When that didn't work, he tried to open it.

It was locked.

Annoyed, he went back to his own room and retrieved his keys. He unlocked the door and said into the darkness beyond, "Felicia."

Still nothing.

His heart suddenly sped up. Had she run away like her brother before her? He perhaps did not *need* an heir of Arthur to make the sword work for him and accomplish his goal of uniting the world under his Command and then invading Faerie – his original plans had not included either of the Knight children since he had not known they existed – but nor did he want them out in the world working against him. Bad enough the brat Wally was at large. If his sister joined forces with him, and with Ariane Forsythe...

He flicked on the light.

A long lump lay in the middle of the king-sized bed. A groan issued from it, resolved into a single grunted word. "What?"

"I told you we have to fly out early," Major said. "You have to get up. The car will be picking us up in twenty minutes."

The lump rolled over. "Go away."

Major walked over to the bed, took hold of the covers, and jerked them down. Felicia, wearing only an over-large T-shirt as a nightgown, shrieked, sat up, and snatched them back up again, holding them to her neck. "How dare you! I'm not dressed!"

"And therein lies the problem," Major said. "*Get* dressed. Now. I presume you packed last night."

"More or less."

"It had better be more than less," Major said. "Because you now have eighteen minutes."

He walked back into the hallway and back to his office to check his email while he waited. His men in Nanaimo had acknowledged receiving his message; they'd be driving down to Victoria that morning to see what was what at the Empress. If they found Ariane's mother, they'd take her to a secure location and let Major know at once.

He nodded in satisfaction. There were also one or two small business matters that required a response; he wrote terse notes dealing with each situation then pushed the chair back from his desk, turned off the monitor, and walked into the living room.

Felicia, looking surly in a blue T-shirt and jeans and bright yellow running shoes, not wearing makeup, and with hair as red as Wally's tied back in a ponytail, stood by the door with a backpack over her shoulder. "Took you long enough," she snarked.

She probably thought that would anger him, but in fact it made him smile. That kind of spirit was exactly what he needed to see in the future leader – *figurehead* leader, but still – of his armies. He looked at her critically. In Arthur's day, it was rare for women to lead armies, but this was a new age. Her face was pretty – at least he thought it was, though he'd never had any interest in the women of Earth, not being human himself, and so was probably not the best judge. Her body he judged likewise attractive by the standards of this age. His marketing people, under his Command, could undoubtedly turn her into the kind of idealized warrior-woman that would have men battling each other for the privilege of fighting under her leadership even *before* she took hold of the hilt of Excalibur and the sword began working its will on those who served its bearer.

He'd seen images of a girl called "Katniss" who featured in popular entertainments about some kind of food competition, although he was unclear on what hunger had to do with warrior women. All the same, the image was compelling. Something along those lines, perhaps.

"The car will be waiting," was all he said out loud. "Let's go."

They rode the elevator down in silence. The silence continued on the trip to the airport through the light traffic of the early-morning darkness. Felicia had been on his private jet before, on the trip from Regina. The minute they were on board, she said, "I'm going back to bed," and started toward the bedroom at the back.

"Wait," Major said.

Felicia halted, heaved an exaggerated sigh, and turned around. "What?"

"Sit down here for a few minutes. I need to tell you what we're doing."

Felicia plopped down on one of the bench seats in the lounge at the front of the plane. "I know what we're doing. We're going to the Caribbean to pick up the fourth shard of Arthur's sword Excalibur. Then we'll find the hilt, and you'll be able to take the other two shards away from that bitch Ariane Forsythe and my stupid little brother, and then you'll make me queen or something. Can I go to bed now?"

"No," Major said. "Buckle up, we're about to take off."

He fastened his own seatbelt as Felicia fastened hers, managing to make even that common-sense safety precaution seem like a horrible imposition. Then he leaned forward.

"I don't know exactly where the shard is on Cacibajagua Island," he said. "I think it's in Jujo Cave, which is a very large sea-cave that has an inland entrance into which empties a freshwater stream. Since the Lady of the Lake would have hid it there, and she can do nothing with salt water, the shard should be near that stream. But over the centuries it could also have moved farther down into the cave."

"If you're about to ask me if I can scuba dive, I can't," Felicia said.

Major, who *had* been about to ask that, tamped down a surge of irritation. "That's all right," he said. "As I said, this is a very large sea cave. It's popular for that very reason: even relatively inexperienced divers can dive it safely. If necessary, we will take scuba-diving lessons so that we can make a guided dive into the cave. I am confident I will sense the shard if we get close enough."

"Sounds like fun," Felicia said, and for once she didn't sound sarcastic.

"It might be," Major said. "However, it also might not be necessary."

They were rolling down the runway. He stopped talking for a moment and forced himself not to clench his hands as the jet angled upward into the night sky.

He hated flying.

Once he heard the whine and thump of the landing gear retracting, and the plane still showed no signs of tipping over and plunging to the ground in fiery ruin, he took a deep breath and continued.

"Cacibajagua Island Diving Adventures also offers submarine tours of the cave," he said. "It is wide enough and deep enough to permit a small submersible to make that journey at high tide. That is how we will begin, shortly after we arrive: I've arranged for a submarine tour of Jujo Cave. That should reveal to me where the shard is hidden. After that, we'll see if we need to dive to retrieve it or if some other method might present itself."

"A sub ride," Felicia said. "Cool. Do they have a pool, too?"

"There's a pool. And a beach."

"Sweet. Cute guys?"

Major sighed. "We will be the only guests. I had my people arrange it. There were a handful of other people staying at the resort, but we have offered them all-expense-paid excursions to the Turks and Caicos for the duration, plus a considerable amount of spending money. I suppose it's possible that some of the *employees* are 'cute guys'...I wouldn't know."

"Too bad," Felicia said. "Now can I go back to sleep?"

"Please."

She unbuckled her seatbelt and headed aft. He stared after her.

He didn't know what to make of the girl. She had spirit, as he'd noted earlier, but she also seemed...willfully obtuse. Unnecessarily confrontational. He knew she was smart – as smart as her brother, Wally, according to the test results he'd arranged to have forwarded to him from Oscana Collegiate in Regina: not just exam marks but personality evaluations and her IQ score – but she hid it all behind the façade of a jaded teenager.

Teenagers had not been recognized as anything special in Arthur's day. Girls Felicia's age – or Ariane's, for that matter – were often already married and mothers. Boys Wally's age would have been apprentices or squires or labourers – not quite the equal of adults because of their smaller size and relative weakness and not given any special consideration. But during this, his second, lifetime on Earth Major had seen youth in general, and teenagers in particular, fetishized to the point of ridiculousness. He didn't understand it. Young people had health and looks going for them, but older people had experience and knowledge.

And power, Major thought. *Don't forget power.*

He got up and moved down the hallway to his on-board office, where he sat at his desk and called up some overseas sales reports he hadn't had a chance to review the day before. He might as well put the three hours to Cacibajagua Island to good use. He'd be busy once he got there.

He smiled as he thought of his men closing in on Ariane's mother, of the submarine tour to come, of the fourth shard of Excalibur he was certain waited for him in Jujo Cave, and of the fact that for once he saw no chance of Ariane and Wally interfering. As Felicia said, he would soon have two of Excalibur's shards, and with her to help him draw power from them, he would soon after have the hilt, and then the entire sword.

He fingered the ruby stud in his earlobe. *Today is going to be a good day,* he thought again, as he had thought the day before.

He set to work.

◄►

"What the *hell?*"

Ariane snapped awake from a troubled dream and stared up, disoriented, at a man silhouetted in a doorway against a grey sky. For an instant she didn't know where she was. The silhouette seemed to have come from her dream, a nasty dream in which the demon Rex Major had once sent to trouble her sleep had returned to chase her once more through the endless woods of those haunted nightmares.

But the figure in the doorway was no demon, she realized as her eyes adjusted. Rather, it was a tall, thin black man wearing white shorts and a white golf shirt with the words "Cacibajagua Island Diving Adventures" neatly stitched over the breast pocket. He stared down at the two of them, without rancor but with enormous confusion; Ariane lying on the floor in her swimsuit and Wally, who, in his trunks beside her, was just then sitting up and blinking.

"Are you guests?" Then he shook his head. "You can't be guests. Rex Major has rented the whole island and sent the other guests packing, and he didn't say anything about you two." He had a strong Jamaican accent.

Ariane's heart rate hadn't settled from the shock of her sudden awakening. The man's mention of Rex Major sent it racing again. "Rex who?" she said, then thought maybe that was a bit over the top – everyone knew who Rex Major was. But she rushed on. "We don't know Rex Major. We're..." she hesitated. They hadn't come up with a cover story. They hadn't intended to be found.

"Shipwrecked," Wally chipped in.

"Shipwrecked?" The man looked bewildered. "What ship?"

"Not really a ship," Wally said. "A boat. A sailing boat. My...sister and I sailed out from...um...Cockburn Town yesterday and, well...we got lost."

Cockburn Town? Ariane stared at Wally. *Is that even a real place?*

"Cockburn?" the man said.

Apparently so.

"Just the two of you?" the man continued.

"Our parents rented the boat," Wally said. "But they were being boring and shopping and we thought we'd just take it out for a spin around the harbour...we've sailed lots back home in Saskatchewan on the lake...and, well, things got out of hand."

"Fog," Ariane said brightly, figuring she ought to say something.

"It *was* grey yesterday," the man said. "Still is." He shook his head. "You were lucky not to drown," he said severely. "Sailing the ocean is not like sailing a lake."

"Don't we know it," Wally said fervently.

"But how did you end up *here?*"

"The boat...capsized," Wally said. "In the dark. We swam ashore. We found the hut, and took shelter. We figured someone would find us in the morning or we could make our way to the resort."

"What happened to your shoulder?"

"During the accident," Wally said. "Hit it on something."

The man shook his head. "Not just lucky," he said. "Protected by God. You should have drowned a dozen times over." He stepped back from the hut door. "Well, get up and come out here."

They stepped outside into the warm grey morning.

Ariane looked around. The sea lay a good three hundred metres away, across a nightmarish tumble of rocks. A light mist kept her from seeing very far out.

So their story was they had somehow managed to swim ashore, then walk across rough rocks without bloodying their bare feet, and by pure happenstance find the only hut on the beach, one which hadn't even had a light on it. Ariane wouldn't have believed it, but on the other hand, she supposed, from the man's point of view, here they were, and how else could they have gotten there?

Just like when I pop into a swimming pool out of nowhere, she thought. *People don't believe in magic, so they'll discount the evidence of their own eyes.*

The cascade poured down the hillside to their right, down from the hilltop lake where they had surfaced when they'd arrived on the island, splashing over black rocks overhung with greenery. Birds chattered and swirled overhead against the leaden overcast.

"It is a half-hour walk back to the resort," the man said, "and I do not recommend it in bare feet."

Since the last place they wanted to go was the resort, Ariane said nothing about the fact they each had a complete change of clothes, including shoes, in their backpacks.

"Fortunately," the man said, "the submarine is headed this way. It carries only two passengers this morning, so there is still room for you. It can surface in the cataract chamber when the tide is mostly in, as it is now, and tie up to the dock. It will get you back to the resort in comfort and then we'll see about getting in touch with your parents and letting them know you're all right."

"Two passengers?" Ariane's heart jumped. "Didn't you just say Rex Major has rented the whole island?"

"Yes, that is right," the man said.

"So one of the passengers is...Rex Major? The...computer guy?"

"Yes," the man said. "You will meet a celebrity. Fortunate yet again."

Ariane swallowed. "And the other passenger?"

The man shrugged. "I do not know her name. A young woman of his acquaintance." His teeth flashed white in a sudden grin. "I am sure Rex Major is always accompanied by a young woman if he chooses to be."

Flish! Ariane exchanged a horrified look with Wally.

"How long until they get here?" said Wally.

"The sub is approaching the underwater entrance of the cave as we speak," the man said. "It must move very slowly, of course, for safety reasons. But it will reach the cascade chamber within forty-five minutes or so. And I must go to prepare the dock." He gave them a stern look. "Stay here," he said. "Do not wander off."

"Wait!" Wally said, as he turned away. "What's your name?"

"Jacob Lewis," the man said. Then he headed down the stairs to the cavern they had explored the day before, unhooking a walkie-talkie from his belt as he went and speaking into it. "You will not believe it," they heard him say. "I have found two children...yes, in the hut...shipwrecked, they say..."

His voice faded.

"At least Rex Major won't be hearing the other end of that conversation if he's already on the way," Ariane said.

"It won't matter if they make us get into a freaking submarine with him – and Flish!" Wally said. "We have to act fast."

"Act how?" Ariane said. The impossibility of the situation struck her again, heavy as a blow to the stomach. "You say the shard is under the rocks, but there's no way we can move them. All Major has to do is Command Jacob and the rest of the resort staff to blow them up, and they'll do it for him. And lock us up somewhere without access to fresh water while they're at it."

"But there *is* something we can do," Wally said urgently. "I thought of it last night."

Ariane stared at him. "What?"

"There's plenty of fresh water in the cavern from the cataract."

"It's already splashing on the rocks. No matter how much force I give it, it won't shift those boulders."

"No, water won't," Wally agreed. "But ice could."

"Ice?" Ariane blinked. "I suppose I could make a lever of ice, but it would just snap. And it's not like I can make a glacier...."

"Ariane, you're not thinking straight," Wally said. "Ice cracks rock all the time. Water expands when it freezes, and almost nothing can stop it. Get fresh water into those rocks, then freeze all the water at once, and the expansion will spread them apart. Do it again, with more water. And again. And before you know it, they're going to crack and tumble...and reveal whatever they're hiding."

"But the shard is under seawater."

"We can dive to get it, as long as we can uncover it," Wally said. "The Lady placed it in the pool, but the rocks must have come down in some earthquake or other. Move them, and we'll see the shard right where she left it."

Ariane felt a flicker of hope. It died almost at once. "But we can't do it now," she said. "We can only do it at low tide. Right now the rocks will be almost completely under seawater. We need to get in there when most of the rocks are uncovered and only the fresh water is pouring down on them." She looked down the stairs. "And Jacob will be back any minute."

"Just because he told us we have to stay put doesn't mean we have to stay put," Wally pointed out. "He's not the boss of us."

Ariane blinked, then laughed. "You're right." Funny

how the feeling she had to do as she was told or get in trouble persisted even now when she was on her own – not to mention being the Lady of the Lake. She looked up at the overcast. "We could go somewhere," she said. "Not too far, because my energy's still low – I need food. Come back at low tide."

"And we need to know when that is," Wally said. "Do you think you could get us to Cockburn Town? We can easily find a tide table there somewhere."

Ariane laughed. "I thought you'd made that name up when I heard you mention it to Jacob. It's a real place?"

He nodded. "It's on Grand Turk Island. Capital of the Turks and Caicos. Pretty much due west of here."

Ariane thought about it for only a moment. "I can do it. But what about Rex Major?" She looked back down into the cavern. "He's about to confirm where the shard is, too."

Wally shrugged. "If it's under all those rocks, it will take him longer to do anything about it than it will take us. Sure, like you said, he could Command the resort staff to blow up the bottom of the cascade – but that means getting them to destroy their main tourist attraction. Even his power may not be up to that task. Or else he'll have to flat out buy the resort for umpteen million dollars and then bring in his own people to demolish the cataract. We've only got to wait a few hours to find out if *our* plan will work. He could be days away from acting."

Ariane held out her hand. "All right," she said. "Cockburn Town it is. We'll get something to eat then wait there until just before low tide, come back to the lake and ride the cataract down again. And then we'll see what we can do." She hesitated. "Those Schisto-things you mentioned..."

"*Schistosoma,*" Wally said. "They're a kind of worm. But you didn't sense them. Just leeches."

"Yeah," Ariane said. "And I'm sure I can make the water keep the leeches off us. So we're good." She reached up for the clouds with her power. She was not as strong as she'd be after she'd eaten, but she could get them to Grand Turk and Cockburn Town.

"Of course, it could be something else, like brain-eating amoeba –" Wally began, but his voice disappeared along with his body.

CHAPTER THIRTEEN

THE SORCERER IN THE SUBMARINE

IN THE SUBMARINE'S CABIN, Rex Major peered up through the curved Plexiglas canopy at the underside of the sea surface. On a sunny day it would have been blue-green and sparkling, but not today, a day so grey it had made their landing on Cacibajagua Island even more knuckle-whitening than an ordinary touchdown. The pilot had assured him that modern navigational equipment and autopilot technology could land the plane safely in an emergency without any pilot input at all, but that had done nothing to reassure Merlin. He knew his fear of flying was irrational, but that was kind of the point, wasn't it? You couldn't be rationally argued out of a position you hadn't been rationally argued into in the first place.

Rationally, he should have been more terrified of a submarine than an airplane. Millions of people flew safely on airplanes every day. Only a relative handful would ever be in a submarine. And personal submarines like the little five-person model he, Flish, and pilot Peter Camus (who also managed the island resort) currently occupied were few and far between.

But he'd never had much fear of drowning. Probably

because, when he had had his full power, it was simply never going to happen. Unlike the Lady of the Lake, he could – or at least *had* been able to – manipulate seawater; he knew its True Name. Had he ever done anything as silly as falling into the ocean, he would simply have formed a bubble of air around himself and risen calmly to the surface.

In any event, and for whatever reason, he found the submarine a fascinating piece of technology. Maybe four and a half metres in length and between two and three metres both tall and wide, it offered a roomy, comfortable cabin where they sat in beige leather seats, complete with armrests and cup holders, while Camus, seated behind them in the centre of the vessel, guided them through the offshore waters of the island to the underwater mouth of the cave.

"It's very unusual for a sea cave to be wide and tall enough for any kind of submarine to pass through it safely," Camus was saying. "But our owner, Mr. Rounsavall, recognized the potential at once. This is our third-generation sub, and the first we've had that can hold five people. Our first two subs only held three."

Dark rock loomed ahead in the headlights' illumination. Camus banked the vessel right, and suddenly the rock vanished, replaced by a black hole that seemed to swallow their lights whole. Camus levelled off, slowed their forward progress, and began easing the sub toward the cave mouth. A school of silvery fish fled their approach.

"Cool," Felicia said from Major's left. He glanced at her. For the first time since he'd healed her leg and taken her from her hospital room to join him in Toronto, she didn't look bored. She sat hunched forward, the red and green lights of the control panel sparkling in her wide eyes.

Major turned his own attention ahead as Camus said, "Of course, we still have to be very cautious. The sub is tough but it wouldn't do to run into a rock at speed."

Major had to agree with that.

They eased at a snail's pace into the cave. Fish of all colours flashed through the lights, and something much bigger and greyer flicked its tail and disappeared before Major got a good look at it. "What was that?"

"Shark," Camus said. "We always make sure the cave is clear of them before we bring tourist divers in here. But we don't have anything to worry about in the sub, of course."

The walls were a riot of colour as well, covered with anemones, corals, and other things Major, whose knowledge of marine biology was practically nil, had no hope of identifying without the running commentary of Camus.

"Big moray eel in that hole there, doesn't look like he's going to show himself today. Those red and white things are flame scallops. We don't actually know what *that* is, but it's pretty, isn't it?"

Major tuned him out, but Felicia drank it all in. "Oh, wow," he heard her murmur once. He glanced at her, and smiled.

But the smile faded as he looked forward again. He wasn't here to sightsee. He had the shard of Excalibur in his pocket. He pulled it out and, as Camus guided them along the cavern with delicate pushes and pulls of the joystick, put it in his left hand and reached it out to Felicia.

She was looking up and didn't see him. He poked her with it. "Hey!" she said, turning angry eyes his way. He jerked a nod at the shard. She glanced down, sighed, and took hold of the other end. Then she turned her attention to the cavern walls again.

Major knew Camus could see what they were doing. He also didn't care. He'd paid so much money to have sole use of the island he was quite certain he could do pretty much anything he wanted without attracting comment.

Merlin had felt nothing from the shard while he held it

in his own hand; Ariane's possessing two of the shards blocked him from accessing its power on his own. But the blood of Arthur ran through Flish's veins as it did through Wally's: the sword, awakened from its long sleep to the possibility of being reforged, would speak to the chosen heirs of the king who had once wielded it just as it would to the Lady of the Lake, whose magic had originally caused it to be made.

Now the barely-there thread of magic that was all he could draw to himself through the almost-closed door into Faerie swelled into a bright rope of power – a faint shadow of what he had once had at his beck and call, but enough to allow him to extend his magical senses beyond the hull of the submarine and into the cavern beyond.

Where he felt...nothing.

In a way, it wasn't a surprise. After researching this place, he'd always thought the most likely location for the shard was the cataract chamber, where fresh water flowed into the sea through the cave's inland entrance.

He kept his senses extended, but still felt nothing, as they continued to crawl through the cavern. It was some seven hundred metres in length, if he remembered accurately – a short walk on the surface, but down here, a half-hour underwater journey.

Looking forward, he saw something new: a glow of light that did not come from the sub's headlights. "Cataract chamber," Camus said. "We're almost there."

The glowing opening drew slowly nearer. Major sat forward, using the power he drew from the shard to reach out with his senses like a snake extending its tongue to taste the air. *It has to be there,* he told himself fiercely. *It has to be!*

And then, abruptly, he felt it, a sudden shock, like the feeling of touching metal on a dry winter's day after shuffling across a carpet.

The fourth shard!

Ahead of them, in the cataract chamber. He was certain of it. And the sense of it was growing stronger – so strong, in fact, that when he pulled the shard of Excalibur free of Felicia's grip – she hardly seemed to notice or care – he could still feel it.

They entered the chamber. He could see the troubled water at the surface, where the waterfall cascaded down from the outside world. Artificial lights made the water sparkle as it had not done in the overcast outside world. Camus turned off the headlights. "We can bring divers in here no matter where we are in the tides," he said, "but the sub can only come in within about an hour and a half either side of high tide, which is around 11:30 a.m. today. The cataract's not quite as spectacular at high tide, of course."

"That's fine," Major said. "I'm happy to see it. We'll be disembarking?"

Camus nodded. "At the dock up ahead. I sent Jacob Lewis around by foot earlier to make everything ready: some bumpers and ropes have to be rigged if we're going to stop here. I can see him up there now." He brought the sub to a halt, though Major could still feel it rising and falling as the water surged around them in response to the distant ocean swell.

"Bit delicate this," Camus said. "Done it before, of course, but it's not something we normally do on the tourist trips; we just come in and turn around and make our way out again. But you said you wanted to see the cataract chamber, so..." He fell silent as he nudged the sub around and reversed it toward the pier. There were a couple of heavy bumps, some scraping noises, and then a sharp rap on the hatch behind them.

"We're tied up," Camus said. "Hold on another minute." He pushed the joystick forward, and the nose of the sub slanted down, though their seats swivelled to remain horizontal. Major looked down past his feet at the bottom of the cavern. There was no riot of sea life in here as there had been in the outer part; mostly, the rocks were bare except for a bit of green fuzz.

The hatch behind them opened. "Welcome to the cataract chamber," a deep voice said.

Major twisted around to see Camus climbing out of his seat to one side, a tight fit because of the various controls; then he folded away his pilot's seat to provide them access to the steep staircase that led up to the outside world. Major got out of his own seat and clambered up that staircase to the boarding platform, complete with handrails, now more-or-less level at the stern of the sub while the bow pointed down. He nodded to a tall, thin black man, and then took a good-sized step upward onto the wooden dock. He turned to help Flish up then went immediately to the railing to look at the cataract.

The tide was now so high the top of the cavern was no more than four metres – on average – from the top of the rising and falling seawater, which sloshed within half a metre or two of the top of the dock. The cataract itself was little more than a brief rush of white foam down black rocks. Major stared at it. Then he turned to Camus and the other man, reached for the thread of power from Faerie, and Commanded, "You will pay no attention to what the girl and I say to each other."

They immediately turned away and began talking to each other as Felicia came up behind him. "Well?" she said, sounding sullen again. Her brief moment of forgetting herself and actually acting like a human being in the submarine was clearly past. "Is it here?"

"It's here," Major said. He shifted his gaze downward, and frowned. "But it's underwater, somewhere. Somewhere deep." He glanced at her. "Listen for it," he said.

"You have Arthur's blood in your veins. You might be able to sense it yourself."

Felicia gave him a skeptical look. But she closed her eyes and cocked her head to one side. After a moment she opened her eyes again. "I can't feel anything."

"Try this," Major said, and held out the shard.

She took the other end, as she had in the sub, and suddenly her eyes widened. "Oh!" she said in wonder. "I *can* feel it! It's like...a spark. Or something."

"Excellent," Major said.

The girl let go of her end of the shard, and Major pocketed it again. Felicia peered down into the water. The submerged lights showed the pile of tumbled rocks at the base of the cataract. "If it's down there, how do we get to it?"

"Are you a good swimmer?" Major said.

Felicia glanced at him skeptically. "Yeah. But I can't dive all the way down there. Not and stay down long enough to do anything."

"Not now," Major said. "But this is high tide. At low tide...perhaps something can be done."

Felicia looked down into the depths again. "If it's buried under those rocks, you'll need dynamite or a backhoe to shift them."

"If that's what it takes, then that is what I'll use," Major said. "But let's not rush to that conclusion. First, we'll wait until low tide. Then you can take a swim and see what's what."

He turned away from the view of the cataract. Behind them Jacob Lewis and Camus were still engaged in muttered conversation. Camus shot a worried look at the cave entrance. "Check the lake," Major heard him say. Lewis nodded and started up the stairs.

The lake? Major frowned. "Is there a problem, Mr. Camus?"

Camus turned toward him. "Nothing important," he

said smoothly – a little too smoothly; Major knew when someone was fudging the truth, and Camus was fudging for all he was worth. "Jacob is concerned about the state of the trail up to Lake Tanama – that's the lake that feeds the cataract – after the storm we had a couple of weeks ago, especially with another storm coming in later today. I've told him to go check it out."

"Uh-huh," Major said. He sighed, and reached again for his thread of power. "Tell me the truth," he Commanded. "What did Jacob Lewis say to you?"

Camus replied at once. "There were two shipwrecked kids in the hut upstairs when Lewis got here this morning," he said. "Teenagers, wearing swimsuits. They said they sailed out of Cockburn Town, got lost, and capsized trying to come ashore here. He said he told them to wait upstairs, but when he went up later, they'd vanished. He's worried they've run into the interior somewhere and he didn't want you to bump into them – I made it very clear to him this morning that nothing was to be allowed to disrupt your visit."

Merlin swore. He didn't do it very often, and the word he used was from Faerie and meant nothing to anyone else on Earth in this age, but it was the worst swearword he knew and he saved it for when he was especially annoyed...which he was now.

Two "shipwrecked" teens who vanished into thin air?

He knew, where magic was involved, coincidences were often nothing of the kind; and where the quest for the shards of Excalibur was concerned, there was no doubt: the two teens could only be Wally and Ariane. Somehow, though he would have sworn it was impossible, they had found out where he was. And if he – and Felicia – could feel the shard down at the bottom of the pool, so could they.

"It was *them*, wasn't it?" Felicia said. "My brother and that bitch."

"Almost certainly," Major said.

"How did they track us to this island?"

"I don't know," Major said, though it galled him to admit it.

"At least they don't have the shard," Felicia said. She glanced back at the cataract. "I can still feel it. It's down there."

"No, they don't," Major said.

"We can't let them have it," Felicia said, and the sudden, angry edge to her voice that made his eyes widen. "It's *mine.*"

Mine, actually, Major thought, but he didn't correct her. *She wants them to fail as much as I do. Maybe even more.*

He snorted. Who was he kidding?

No one wanted Wally and Ariane to fail as much as he did.

"They won't get it," he said out loud. "Powerful though the Lady of the Lake has made Ariane, she can do nothing with salt water. They have no way to retrieve it."

"Do you?" Felicia said.

"Maybe," Major said. "As I said, if I have to, I'll Command that the cavern be blasted apart. But I may not need to. I may have another way. Before we take any action, though, we need to be completely sure where the shard is, and how deeply buried." He released the thread of power, and Camus blinked. He wouldn't remember what he'd just told them. "This cavern is fascinating," Major said, as if he had just turned back to Camus, "but I'd really like to see it at low tide. Can we come back then?"

"Sure," Camus said. "But not by sub. I think you said neither of you are trained divers?"

"That's right," Major said. "And I don't imagine six hours is enough to learn."

Camus smiled. "No. We offer a learn-to-dive package

that culminates with a guided dive into the cave, but it's a week-long program. But if you just want to see the cataract chamber at low tide, you can walk here from the resort. There's a path that follows the shoreline. Or if you prefer the scenic route, you can hike up to the top of the hill to see Lake Tanama, and then come down a rather steep trail that parallels the stream."

Major smiled. "We'll follow the shore, thanks."

"Do you want to walk there now, or take the sub back?"

"We'll walk," Major said. "To be sure we know the way."

"Well, you can't really miss it." Camus pointed up the steps. "Go up there, you'll see the start of the path. It's level and paved with crushed stone, and there are board-walks that take you over some lovely tidal pools."

"How long a walk?"

"About half an hour."

"So we'll have a few hours at the hotel?" Felicia put in. Major glanced at her. "Why?"

"There's a pool," Felicia said. "With a floating bar. And a cute bartender."

Camus laughed. "That's Felipe. He'll be happy to have the company, since there's no one else at the resort."

"Very well," Major said. "Come along, Felicia. Thank you, Mr. Camus."

He led his young charge up the stairs to the platform at the top. There was a small hut there, probably for equipment. The path to the hotel began with a railless boardwalk bridge, wet with spray, under which the stream tumbled into the darkness of the cave. On the other side, a signpost pointed up the hillside: "To Tanama Lake." Lewis was already a hundred yards along the path, toiling upwards.

Major watched him climb. He didn't think that Wally and Ariane were still on the island. They would have left, gone somewhere out of easy reach, to plan. And he thought he knew what that plan had to be. They had seen how inaccessible the fourth shard was. Ariane could do nothing with salt water. They would scheme instead to somehow steal the shard from him after he had done whatever was necessary to retrieve it, as they had done once before, in Yellowknife. But they didn't know that he knew that they knew he was here. He knew the precautions to take. They would not, *could not* succeed.

And if things went well in Victoria...

He smiled, then. The fourth shard was a prize, to be certain, and he would claim it: but it also made excellent bait for a trap. If – *when* – Wally and Ariane showed up, he would spring that trap, and put an end to this tiresome charade once and for all.

He pulled out his smartphone. Felicia gave him a scornful look. "You don't really think you're going to get a signal out here, do you?"

"Actually, I'm certain of it," Major said. "Didn't you read the welcome brochure in your room? You can use your phone anywhere. At ruinous expense, of course, but the people who come to private islands for vacations don't usually care about the expense. And people like me, who rented the whole island, *really* don't care."

"Dammit," Felicia muttered. "If I'd known, I wouldn't have left mine in my room."

Major checked his email. Nothing yet from Victoria, but it was still early there. And they had six hours before low tide. Wally was smart: he'd have figured out that the best time for Major to try to retrieve the shard would be then. That was when Ariane and Wally would show up. And that would be when the trap would spring, if all went well.

He tucked the phone back into his pocket. "Let's hurry along, shall we?"

But despite the pleasures awaiting her at the hotel, Felicia hesitated. "You're sure you're not worried about Wally and Ariane? You don't want to stay here in case they turn up?"

Again, Major felt a flash of approval. "Commendable thinking," he said, "but I don't think we have to worry about them for a while. And I wouldn't dream of depriving you of your rendezvous with the floating bartender." He indicated the path. "After you, milady."

Felicia actually grinned at that, and set off along the path to the resort.

CHAPTER FOURTEEN

LIGHTNING AND ICE

Some six hours after they had left Cacibajagua Island, Ariane and Wally returned, materializing in a fountain of spray at the edge of Lake Tanama just as they had the night before, but this time in daylight – though just barely: sunset was only an hour away and the sky remained overcast.

They'd spent the intervening time in Cockburn Town on Grand Turk Island, a pleasant place with low-rise brightly coloured buildings and old-fashioned lampposts. Despite the grey weather, it had been heavily infested with tourists from two giant cruise ships currently in port. The crowds had suited Wally and Ariane just fine, since they'd blended right in even in their swimsuits. They'd bought food, they'd bought more bottled water to take with them back to Cacibajagua – Ariane could probably purify water to make it safe to drink, but bottled water was easier, and Wally's mention of brain-eating amoeba had disinclined Ariane to experiment – and they'd talked about their plan.

Wally's plan, really.

"At low tide, most of those rocks at the base of the cataract are going to be exposed, and the water running over them and between them will be fresh water," he said, as they sat by the beach eating jerk chicken from a nearby beach bar. "Freeze what's there, and keep freezing the water that flows in from the cataract, and those boulders will shift. Especially since you can freeze the water *instantly*. That's a lot of force."

"You have a lot of confidence in my abilities," Ariane mumbled around a mouthful of chicken. It really was the best chicken she'd ever eaten. The virgin cocktail at her right hand was also delicious, once you fought your way past the umbrella and fruit slices decorating the edge of the fake-coconut cup.

"If I may quote something someone said to me recently," Wally said, "you're the freaking Lady of the Lake."

Ariane laughed, but she wasn't nearly as certain as Wally that what he was suggesting would work. Yes, she'd frozen water in small amounts – but freezing that much, and that quickly? Could she do it? Would she have the power?

"I'll need your help," she said. "I'll need all the power I can get. That means drawing on the shard, with you holding it. Just like when we crossed the Pacific from New Zealand."

Wally nodded seriously. "I'll be right there at your side," he said, taking her hand. "Always."

She'd squeezed his hand in return, and then kept holding it, because it felt good. A matronly woman passing by in a broad-brimmed white hat and a brightly coloured muumuu had given them an indulgent smile. Ariane had smiled back.

Now she and Wally, holding hands again, waded out of Tanama Lake in roughly the same place they'd come ashore the night before. She shuddered a little at the thought of the leeches, even though her power had sent them all tumbling away from them through the water. She shuddered more at the thought of brain-eating amoeba, even though Wally had apologized for mentioning them and assured her he didn't *really* think the lake was infested with them. Once on land, she ordered them both dry. They still wore their swimsuits, but they'd each pulled a T-shirt on over top and put on their runners without socks to protect their feet. Ariane's T-shirt was black, her preferred colour: Wally's, a spare one he'd had in his backpack, was another in the seemingly endless series of geeky shirts that made up the bulk of his wardrobe. This one was leaf-green and bore a single phrase in block letters: I AM GROOT.

The overcast had, if anything, thickened, the clouds lower than that morning and moving swiftly across the sky. Though sheltered where they stood, she could hear wind hissing through the trees. Palm fronds swayed high overhead. Wally looked up. "Storm's coming in."

"But you said it's not a hurricane, right?" Ariane said anxiously. She'd always had a fear of hurricanes, a pretty irrational one considering she'd lived her whole life thousands of kilometres inland. Oddly enough, she didn't really worry about tornadoes, even though the worst tornado disaster in Canadian history had actually occurred in her hometown of Regina. That had been well over a century ago, though.

"The forecast wasn't calling it a hurricane. And officially, hurricane season ended November 30. But it's way more than an ordinary thunderstorm. And it's really unusual to have this kind of cloud cover in the Caribbean, lasting for so long."

Ariane stared up at the clouds again. How much of this weird weather was due to chance, and how much was the insidious working of magic from Faerie? She remembered another extraordinary bit of luck, the cruise ship in whose pool she'd materialized when she'd been on the verge of falling from the sky into the sea on her way back from France. She'd felt more than once that the shards wanted to be found by her rather than Major. Could the Lady's magic exert power even over the weather?

She knew it could: she'd made it snow in Regina the first time she'd reached up to the clouds.

It should have been reassuring to think that somehow her power was aiding her in ways she didn't even realize – but it wasn't, not entirely, because if her magic had something to do with these clouds, it was magic that was happening outside her control. And that made her wonder how much control she really had over any of the events into which she'd been plunged. Was she really the Lady of the Lake, a queen on the chessboard, or just a pawn in some greater game?

She shook her head. *Or maybe,* she thought, *it just happens to be a cloudy day.*

They'd timed their return to give them almost an hour until low tide. Their last plunge into the salt water of the cavern had been out of control and dangerous. This time they intended to walk down – if they could.

"There has to be a path down to the cavern from the lake," Wally had reasoned while they were holding hands on the beach at Cockburn Town. "We just couldn't see it in the dark."

Now here they were in the light, and once again, Wally's reasoning proved sound. A path circled the lake. They'd followed it before to a platform that overlooked the sea and the falling stream, and when they returned to that platform, they saw below them the hut where they'd spent the night and the entrance to the cavern. But now they could also see the other end of the path round the lake, just on the other side of the waterfall at their feet, the start of a steep switch-backing trail down the hillside. "Joju Cave," read a signpost.

Looking down, Ariane saw that a boardwalk bridge crossed the stream just above where it fell into the cavern. A well-marked path then continued along the seashore, presumably all the way to the resort. "Where do you suppose Rex Major is?" she said uneasily. "We're going to be awfully exposed on that trail."

"No way to tell," Wally said. "But my guess is he's at the resort, probably Commanding left, right, and centre, telling them to bring in heavy equipment and explosives. It won't be easy even with his magic to get them to destroy their major attraction. With luck, it'll keep him too busy to bother us."

Luck, Ariane thought. *There's that word again.* She looked up at the clouds. *If the power of the Lady can influence the world to that extent – if it really has anything to do with the weather that made it easier for us to get here – can it also influence Rex Major?*

No, she decided. *His magic is at odds with the Lady's. He has power, too, more than before, thanks to the shards returning to the world and his possession of one...and with Flish to help him. If the Lady's magic is helping us all the way from Faerie, it's doing it in subtle ways. And it will take something far from subtle to influence Merlin.*

"Then let's get moving," she said.

They hurried around the small lake, reaching the head of the path down to the cavern in about fifteen minutes. The trail proved to be every bit as steep as it had looked, but at least it wasn't slippery and half-covered in snow like the one they'd twice descended to Horseshoe Bay. Ariane blinked in astonishment: had that really just been *yesterday?*

It had. It seemed a lifetime.

The wind grew stronger as they neared the cavern, and as they reached the top of the stairs lightning flickered out over the ocean. Several seconds later Ariane heard a low grumble.

"Storm's coming," Wally said, staring out at sea. "And look at the surf."

The waves had grown angry in the short time it had taken them to descend from Lake Tanama. The sea hurled itself against the rocks, exploding in huge fountains of white spray.

"Shouldn't bother us in the cave," Ariane said.

"No," Wally said. "Although it may increase the swell." He took another long look out to sea before ducking into the hut to turn on the lights inside the cavern; with sunset just minutes away and the clouds so thick, it was already getting hard to see. Then he followed Ariane down into the cataract chamber.

The seawater inside had receded an astonishing amount, uncovering almost all of the tumbled boulders at the base of the cataract. "I can feel it now even from here," Wally said, staring at the fresh water cascading over the rocks. "Stronger than ever."

"I still can't feel it at all," Ariane said. "Are you sure?"

"I'm sure." Wally turned wide eyes to her. "You really can't feel it, and I can?"

She nodded, feeling irritated. "Yeah. Really."

"It must still be under the salt water." He checked his watch. "It's not quite low tide, but it won't go out much more. I think you should get started."

Ariane nodded. She'd thought about how to approach the task, and realized the only way she could bring the necessary power to bear was to be as close to the water as possible. She didn't think she could use her power at all if she were in the salt water, but she didn't think she could do what she needed to do from the dock, either. And she needed Wally with her if she was going to make good use of the shard she wore against her skin, beneath her swimsuit. "Let's do it."

Side by side, they pulled off their T-shirts and shoes,

and stuffed them into their backpacks. Ariane swung herself off onto the ladder and descended to the seawater. Wally followed her down.

"Nice and warm," he said, treading water.

"It's disgusting," she said between clenched teeth. "Let's get out of here." She set out across the pool in a splashy front crawl. She hated the touch of the sea more than ever. It seemed *wrong*. It felt like water, it moved like water, but she could do nothing with it. It not only resisted her, it seemed to actively dislike her. But it was only water, all the same, and even though it made her skin squirm, she could swim in it.

A minute later she hauled herself out onto the rocks down which the cascade tumbled. Wally climbed out after her. She plunged her head into the wonderfully fresh water. She felt her power roar up within her, the shard she wore against her skin blazing like a star in her inner sight.

Oops. The shard. Wally had to hold it if she were going to draw on its power. And she'd cleverly put it underneath her swimsuit. Which meant...

She sighed. "Turn your back," she said.

"What?"

"Turn your back," she said. "The shard is under my swimsuit. I'm going to have to peel it down to get to it. Turn your back."

"Oh!" Wally blushed, and since he was only wearing swim trunks, she could see that the blush went all the way to his belly button. "Sorry!"

He hastily turned his back. Ariane turned her back on him, too, peeled the suit half-off, pulled out the shard, and then tugged the swimsuit back into place. "All right," she said.

He turned around again. Ariane, using the shard of Excalibur like a pointer, indicated the top of the pile of stones, right where the water poured in. "I think we need to be up there," she said. "Come on."

She began picking her way up the slippery rocks. Although nothing very big grew on them, probably because they alternated between being covered with fresh water and being covered with salt, clearly something microscopic had enthusiastically colonized them and set about busily producing that favorite product of all things bacterial: slime. As she and Wally climbed, she saw a flicker of lightning in the hole in the cave ceiling, lighting up the darkening sky, followed by a grumble of thunder.

She only slipped badly once, her foot going out from under her, and Wally grabbed her ankle and guided her toes back to safety before she lost her grip completely. She took a deep breath, glanced back with a smile, and then continued climbing.

At the top of the rocks the ceiling of the cave closely overhung a kind of ledge. The overhang was too low to let them sit on the ledge, but they could lie down on it, side by side – though just barely. With Wally's body pressed against hers, Ariane took hold of the shard and had him take hold of the other end.

Instantly the power she had at her call expanded, the feeling so sudden she gasped with pleasure. *I can do this,* she said. *I know I can.*

She closed her eyes, and concentrated.

She didn't want to freeze the water up here, where it continued to pour in, flashes of lightning from the approaching storm illuminating it as though paparazzi stood just outside the cave taking photos. The freezing had to happen down below, in the myriad cracks and crevices and gaps between the boulders: and it had to happen suddenly. Instantly. She let the strange sense that told her exactly where water was and how it would behave take over. There, she thought. *There, there, there, and...there.*

She seized power from within herself, and from the

shard, and hurled it into the pile of stones.

A deafening crack, far louder than the thunder outside, reverberated around the cavern. Two smaller stones burst from the pile as if punched by the fists of trolls, and hurtled into the middle of the cave, splashing into the heaving salt water. The entire pile groaned.

Ariane kept her eyes closed. New gaps had opened. More water poured into them. Once again she exerted her power. Once again the water flashed to ice, expanding as it did so. And once again, as it did all over the world, as it always had, the rock, not the ice, gave way. The pile of stones grumbled, shifted. A boulder half as big as Wally burst loose and crashed downhill, hitting the water with a splash that hurled wavelets against all the walls of the cavern.

More water, more ice, more cracking of stones, more tumbling boulders. The entire pile groaned and shifted. Now the cascade hardly poured down the outside of the rocks at all. Instead, it drained into the interior of the pile, puddling on the ice Ariane had already formed, filling every cubic centimetre of open space. She waited...waited...waited until the water was everywhere in the pile, until it began spilling out – and then, once more, she thrust power into the heap.

As though a bomb had detonated inside the pile, boulders burst from the places they had lain for centuries, tumbled and rolled and banged and thudded and splashed. And then Ariane did it again. And again. And then...

And then, suddenly, at last, *she felt the shard.* Somewhere at the bottom of the pile, the shifted boulders had dammed the seawater, allowing a pool of fresh water to form, and that fresh water at last, at long, long last, had come in contact with the fourth shard. It sang in her mind, joyful to be found, joyful that *she*, heir to the Lady of the Lake who had had it forged, had found it. She tried to pull it to her, to make the water lift it to her side, but she couldn't. "Wally," she gasped out, without opening her eyes, not wanting to spoil the moment, "it's exposed. I can feel it. Can you get down there, free it, get it for me?"

But Wally didn't respond. She felt him tense beside her, heard him mutter a swearword – and then he released the shard, so suddenly she gasped as her access to its power vanished, and scrambled up and over her. "What – ?" Her eyes jerked open to see him climbing up the rocks, out of the cave, the cataract pouring around his slim white body, lit by a brilliant flash of lightning just before he disappeared entirely into the dimming twilight.

Then she looked down at the dock and saw what he had seen and, like the water she had manipulated moments before, her blood turned to ice.

Rex Major stood there. Beside him was Flish, barely dressed in a blue bikini, a towel around her neck, staring at Ariane with undisguised glee and hatred.

Beside *them* stood Lewis, his face strangely blank. He had a gun in his hand.

"Get the boy," Major snarled, and Lewis lifted the pistol and ran for the stairs.

CHAPTER FIFTEEN

GUNFIRE AND THUNDER

IF WALLY WERE PERFECTLY HONEST with himself, the best part of the effort to free the fourth shard of Excalibur from its stony prison was the chance to lie crammed up against Ariane in the cozy confines of the little crevice into which she'd tucked herself while she worked her magic. *You're a walking cliché of a teenage boy, aren't you?* he told himself. *All you can think about is –*

Magic! He gasped as he felt it drawn from the shard he held with Ariane. And then he saw the white crystals of ice erupt between the boulders below them, and saw two small rocks hurtle across the chamber, and forgot everything else as he marvelled at what Ariane could do – *was doing* – even though he'd suggested it.

The jumbled boulders, tons of rock, came apart like a pile of blocks kicked over by an impatient toddler. He didn't need Ariane to tell him when the fourth shard was at last exposed: he'd been feeling its presence since they returned to the chamber, but that had been like distant sheet lightning from the approaching storm – the moment it was truly revealed, it blazed in his mind like a bolt striking directly overhead.

And then he saw Rex Major and Flish and Jacob Lewis walk out onto the dock.

He swore. Then he did the only thing he could think to do.

He ran.

He scrambled over top of Ariane, got onto the rocks, and climbed up and out of the cavern, the water foaming around him. Once outside, he stumbled to the bank to his left and scrambled out of the water.

The wind had howled to a gale and the lighting flickered constantly, but the storm hadn't truly broken yet – the thunder still lagged the lightning by several seconds, grumbling distantly instead of shattering the sky.

He glanced behind him. Lewis charged into the open at the top of the stairs, gun in hand. Wally gulped and dashed across the path, hoping to lose the skinny black man in the jungle. But as he plunged in among the wind-whipped trees, he heard a flat cracking sound that definitely wasn't thunder, and something tore a chunk out of the trunk of a palm tree just above his head. He flung himself to the ground, gasping.

Lewis had shot at him. Lewis had actually *shot* at him!

And just like that, his fear vanished, swallowed up in an immense, burning anger, a rage both hot as a lightning bolt and as cold as the ice Ariane had conjured below. The heat of that fury drove him to do what he did next; but the ice told him how to do it.

Flat on his belly, he wriggled through the heaving trees, not away from the cave, but back toward it. He could see the boardwalk over the cataract through the leaves. He saw Lewis dash across it, saw him slow as he reached the footpath and drew closer to the spot where Wally had disappeared.

And then the man was within reach.

Wally exploded from hiding like an attacking jungle

cat. He leaped up and slammed into Lewis. Lewis was much taller and outweighed him by a considerable amount, but even the biggest man would go down if hit properly, and Wally crashed into him like a defensive back taking down a receiver, right at the knees. Lewis cried out and fell, the gun flying from his hand. Wally leaped over him, rolled across rock, picking up new cuts and bruises, feeling the wound in his shoulder tear open anew, but coming up with the gun.

Lewis froze as Wally aimed the pistol at him. He'd never even held one before, and it felt alien in his hand, far heavier than he'd expected. Yet somehow he knew, if he chose to fire, he would not miss. "I know it's not your fault," Wally growled at Lewis. "You're under Merlin's Command. But I can't let you stop us."

Lewis said nothing. He hardly seemed to hear Wally. Maybe he couldn't, under Merlin's Command. He simply ignored the gun and leaped.

Wally's finger started to tighten on the trigger – then something inside him rebelled, pushed back at the sword-fed impulse to kill. Instead he dodged, the shard's power making him far fleeter of foot than the man. The gun seemed to reverse itself in his hand without his thinking about it, and he brought the handle down on Lewis's head, just above the ear.

Lewis went down like he'd been clubbed – which, of course, he had – and didn't move. A trickle of blood flowed from the cut the gun had opened.

Wally threw the gun into the jungle, then ran for the stairs, as lightning exploded directly overhead in the now-black sky, and the crack of thunder hard on its heels brought the storm down upon the island in earnest.

◀▶ ▶

As Lewis dashed up the stairs and into the gathering storm in pursuit of the vanished Wally, Ariane kept her eyes on Merlin.

"I want to thank you for this," the sorceror said. He indicated the scattered and shattered boulders. "I'd hoped you'd solve this problem for me. I had some ideas of my own, but having you do the work that hands me the fourth shard...well, I couldn't have asked for anything better."

Ariane looked at Flish. "Rex Major just sent a man with a gun after your brother. Doesn't that bother you at all?"

Flish laughed. "He's not going to shoot him. Just catch him."

At that moment, a gunshot echoed through the cave from outside, loud even above the sound of water and wind and grumbling thunder. Ariane's heart leaped in her chest. *Wally!*

Flish, eyes suddenly wide, shot a shocked glance at Rex Major.

"He won't kill him," Major said. "That was just a warning shot. I'm sure Lewis will bring Wally back safe and sound in a few minutes." He jerked his head at the water. "Get in there and get that shard. It's exposed. I can feel it."

Flish looked at the cave opening uncertainly a moment longer; then she took a sudden sharp breath and turned toward the pool. "So can I," she breathed.

What? Ariane stared at the older girl, feeling outrage. Flish flashed Ariane a mocking smile, then climbed down the ladder into the water.

The cataract still poured around Ariane. The moment Wally had fled, she'd lost the extra power his touch on the shard gave her – and discovered just how much of her *own* power she'd been pouring into her ice-making.

She felt exhausted, hammered flat, as if the boulders she'd forced out of their spots had fallen upon her instead of into the sea. She wanted to seize the water flowing past her, hurl it at Rex Major as a weapon, hurt him, drive him to his knees, kill him if she could...

But she couldn't. She had almost nothing left. She needed time to rest, to regenerate.

And she wasn't going to get it.

Below her, Flish pulled herself dripping out of the water, and knelt among the rocks Ariane's magic had shifted. Her hand plunged into the turbulent pool of fresh water into which the cataract now fell before pouring over the dam of boulders into the seawater.

And came out holding the fourth shard of Excalibur.

It was the twin of the third shard, a piece of metal perhaps twenty centimetres long, with a groove down its middle. Ariane heard its song crescendo as Flish pulled it out – but that swelling power was not directed at her. She could do nothing with it. Instead, it was at the beck and call of...

Her gaze jerked back to the dock.

Merlin.

"I must say," Rex Major called, "I am impressed you were able to trace me here." Wearing a Tilley hat, a loose-fitting flowered Hawaiian-style shirt, loose khaki pants and sandals, he looked every inch a vacationing business-man rather than an ancient, ruthless, and alien magician. He leaned casually on the railing of the dock.

"When I heard about the two 'shipwrecked' teens mysteriously found in the hut up above, who then even more mysteriously disappeared, I knew immediately it was you and Wally. And while I understand how you knew Felicia and I were visiting the Caribbean, I am quite astonished you managed to make the leap from 'Caribbean' to Cacibajagua Island." He looked thoughtful for a moment. "I don't really care to be astonished. Would you like to tell me how you did it?" When Ariane made no answer, he sighed. "Never mind. You'll tell me later."

"No," Ariane said, trembling with fatigue. "I won't."

Felicia's attention had remained tightly focused on Ariane. Now she chimed in with, "Yes, you will, you bitch. We've got two shards now, and we'll find the hilt."

"You can't take my shards from me," Ariane said. "You can't kill me. You can't hold me. I can vanish in an instant."

"Without Wally?" Flish said, her voice dripping with venom. "You two made it yet or has he realized what a skank you are?"

Fury roared up in Ariane at her words, fury fed by the shard she still held in her hand. Despite her exhaustion, tentacles of water rose up around Felicia, turned to ice-tipped spears. "Give me the shard," she snarled. "Give it to me, and maybe *I* won't kill *you.*"

Flish's eyes widened. She froze in place.

"Tsk," Merlin said. He sounded bored. "You shouldn't try to threaten. You don't do it very well." He dug into his pocket, pulled out a smartphone. "Did you know they have cell phone service on this island?" he said conversationally. "They've really spared no expense." He poked at the screen. "I know it's kind of noisy in here, but you can probably hear this." He held up the phone, screen toward her. "Mr. Axelrod," he said loudly. "Please tell the young lady what you've done today."

"Just like you said, Mr. Major," came a voice, tinny and thin, but still somehow carrying above the rush of water from the cataract – boosted, no doubt, by some small magical trick of Merlin's. "We drove down to Victoria from Nanaimo. We found Emily Forsythe working in the Tea Lobby at the Fairmont Empress. Grabbed her on her coffee break. She's safely tucked away. We're just awaiting further orders."

"Just hold her, Mr. Axelrod," Major said. "Until I tell

you otherwise."

"As you say, Mr. Major."

Major drew back the phone, turned it off.

The rush of water all around Ariane faded to nothing beneath the roaring of the blood in her veins.

"I'm sure you understood what that meant," Major said. "I've found your mother, Ariane. I'm holding her prisoner. You have no way of knowing where."

"Ha!" said Flish. "Didn't see that coming, did you?"

Major held up a hand to quiet the girl. To Ariane he said, "And unless you hand over the shards of Excalibur you possess, immediately and of your own free will, I will have her killed. Am I clear?"

The tentacles of ice-tipped water surrounding Flish fell splashing into the pool. Ariane hardly noticed. All her attention had turned inward. Deep inside herself she found the tendril of power that led from her to her mother, the thread of shared magic that had linked them, heart to heart, when at last they had come face to face – the thread that had remained constantly humming with life at the core of her being every moment since.

They were both heirs of the Lady of the Lake. Ariane had accepted the power though her mother had not, but her mom still held a portion of it – and Ariane discovered, in that moment of need, that she could draw on her mother's power as well as her own, at least for one thing:

To go to her.

She forgot all about the shards of Excalibur. She forgot all about Major, all about Flish, all about Wally.

The cataract chamber of Joju Cave vanished from around Ariane in an instant as she dissolved into the water of the cataract and then leaped up into the lightning-riven clouds.

No one threatened her mother.

No one!

Few things could surprise Merlin after two lifetimes on Earth and many, many long years before that in Faerie, but Ariane's disappearance after he issued his threat managed it. He gaped at the spot where she had been until, suddenly, she wasn't. *She must be going back to Victoria,* he thought. *But she doesn't know where my men are holding her mother. I don't even know – I made* sure *I didn't know.*

Instinct. That had to be it. Her mother having been threatened, she'd run off to try to save her, even though it was futile. She'd clearly been exhausted. She wouldn't even have the power to *get* to Victoria, and fast though she seemed to be able to get around, it would surely take her a couple of hours at least.

Even if she got there, it wouldn't change anything. She couldn't find her mother. She would come crawling back to him soon enough, not only willing but eager, *desperate,* to give him the two shards she still held.

By which time he would *also* have two. The ice-tipped tentacles of water that had been threatening Felicia had fallen away. "What are you waiting for?" he shouted. "Bring me the shard."

Felicia, who had been staring in astonishment at the spot from which Ariane had vanished, turned toward him. "How did she...?"

"Really? You still have to ask?" Major said. "Magic, you stupid girl. I would have thought by now you'd figured out it's real. Now bring me the shard!" The shard was right there, but not in his grasp. It was infuriating – but even as the sharp reply left his lips, he regretted it: he needed Felicia's good will, and he could no more Command her than he could her brother, thanks to the blood of Arthur in their veins. "I'm sorry," he called at once. "I'm just anxious. Please, Felicia, hurry."

There, that was better, though from the look the girl gave him, not much. Something had changed: her face held a wariness that hadn't been there since he had healed her leg. "You said you'd kill her mom," she said slowly. "I mean, I hate her, but...that's *murder.*"

Major felt contempt. *And murder is a step too far for you?* he thought. *We'll have to change that if you're going to be my warrior queen.*

But for now...

He composed his face into an expression of innocence. "It was just a threat. I have no intention of killing her mother, or anyone else. But I had to find a way to get her to stand down before she hurts someone...or gets hurt herself."

He saw the doubt fading from Flish's face. *She wants to believe,* he thought. *And that's almost as powerful a force as the Voice of Command.* "And it worked. Ariane's gone. Now bring me the shard. That's why we're here."

"Yeah," Flish said. And, at last, she moved. She waded back into the seawater, looked doubtfully at the shard, looked down at herself, tucked the shard carefully into the waistband of her bikini bottom, and then finally – *finally*, while Major maintained his reasonable expression through sheer force of will – launched herself into the water and started swimming toward the dock.

Major went to the ladder to meet her. From behind him he heard the slap of bare feet running on wood and half-turned – then fell head over heels into the seawater of Joju Cave as Wally Knight slammed into him at a dead run.

◄◄ ►►

Wally had dashed headlong back toward the cave, leaving Jacob Lewis bleeding and unconscious on the trail behind him. The rain arrived as he reached the top of the wooden steps leading down into the cataract chamber, pouring down with sudden force as though the whole sky had become a waterfall. Wally ignored it, as he ignored the lightning and thunder and the pain of his cuts and bruises. He knew Rex Major would expect Lewis to bring him back. *Dead or alive,* he thought angrily. Standing over the black man's body, he'd been able – barely – to withstand Excalibur's urging him to kill Lewis. But the fury still fulminated inside him, some of it his, some of it the sword's, and he could no longer tell which was which.

But angry didn't have to mean stupid. He crept down the stairs to the very edge of the platform.

He could see Rex Major's back, where the sorcerer stood pressed against the railing, as though it were between him and the one thing he loved most in the world – which, clearly, it was. He couldn't see his sister, but he could hear her voice, asking a question, though between the rush of the water in the cavern and the rush of wind and rain and thunder outside he couldn't understand what it was. If Ariane were still in the cavern, she wasn't talking.

But he was plenty close enough to Rex Major say, "Now bring me the shard." He sounded like a man coaxing a dog that was reluctant to bring back the stick he'd thrown for it. "That's why we're here," he added.

Even through his anger, Wally's mind remained wondrously clear, his thoughts arraying themselves in perfect order, like bullets in a magazine. What Major had just said meant Flish was down in the water – and *she had the shard.* She *had it...not Major.*

And Major, who had Commanded an innocent man to come after Wally with a gun, had just moved to the top of the ladder, the only part of the platform that didn't have a railing, to help Felicia climb out.

Without thinking, it seemed, or else thinking thoughts shaped and sharpened by Excalibur itself, Wally hurtled across the platform and slammed into the centuries-old sorcerer who had threatened him and the girl he loved.

He hit him low and hard. Merlin toppled into the water, and Wally followed him.

Still driven by the strange, sharp knowledge of exactly what he needed to do, Wally twisted like a fish the moment he hit the sea and struck out for his sister, who had stopped in the middle of the cave, treading water, her eyes wide. He knew she had the shard on her and it wasn't in her hand, so it had to be in her swimsuit. He dove beneath the surface, and saw it glimmering against the skin of her left flank. She tried to twist out of his way, but like his thoughts, his swimming ability had grown sharp as the shard itself. He snatched it from the waistband of her bikini, feeling cloth give as he did so, and struck out for where the water of the cataract foamed against the surface of the seawater.

She grabbed his foot, but he kicked, hard, and broke free. A moment later he was clambering out onto the boulders of the cataract, and climbing out of the cave, rain and wind in his face, lightning splitting the sky, thunder cracking and growling and rumbling. He glanced back. Felicia remained in the water, screaming at him, though he couldn't hear her; for some reason she hadn't tried to follow him up the rocks. Major floundered his way back to the ladder.

Wally knew exactly where he had to go with the shard: up the zigzagging path to Lake Tanama. Wherever Ariane had gone, she would be back for him, and she would appear in the lake. He only had to keep out of Merlin's clutches until that happened, and then Ariane would have her three shards – and Major would be *done*. With the power of three shards, Ariane would be unstoppable. They'd have the hilt within days, and take Merlin's shard from him soon after.

He reached the path and ran, the rain still pouring down in sheets, sluicing around his body. His wounded shoulder ached. The stones, sharp beneath his feet, had to be cutting them, too, but pain seemed unimportant with the shard in his hand. He felt nothing but strength and razor-sharp mental clarity.

Lewis no longer lay where he had fallen; presumably he'd woken up, and, free of Command and no doubt horribly confused as well as injured, staggered back toward the resort.

Wally reached the bottom of the lake trail, now its own mini-cataract: water poured down it, lit every few seconds by flares of lighting. He didn't hesitate: he knew he had the skill to climb it, knew he would not slow or slip until he reached the top, knew that his plan was sound and Ariane would be back for him, knew it all with an absolute confidence that would have seemed utterly foreign to the Wally Knight who had begun the Lady's quest, or even the Wally Knight who had arrived on the island just a little over an hour earlier – but *that* Wally seemed to have vanished, subsumed by this new, improved version: less Wally, a lot more Knight.

He glanced back as he reached the first switchback in the path, to see Merlin at the top of the stairs, Flish with him, a towel wrapped around her waist. He resumed climbing, reached the second switchback, glanced back again to see Merlin and Flish at the bottom of the path. But Major stopped Flish there. He was shouting up at Wally, Wally could see that, but he couldn't hear the sorcerer, and he didn't care. They couldn't catch him, and he could elude them forever in the jungle covering the island – or for at least as long as he had to, until Ariane came back.

And she *would* come back. For the shard, and for him. He was certain of that, too.

He reached the third switchback, the last place from which the bottom of the path was still visible before trees hid it.

The world turned white.

Wally felt himself flying through the air, head ringing like a hammer-struck bell...

...and then the world faded from white to black.

CHAPTER SIXTEEN

THE WATERWOMAN AND MERLIN'S RAGE

ARIANE HAD NEVER TESTED exactly how fast she could move through cloud and stream using the Lady's power. She knew it was faster than the fastest plane, but it had always taken a significant amount of time, nonetheless, to cover a long distance: hours across the oceans, even if far fewer than a jetliner. From Cacibajagua Island to Victoria was a very long way indeed – and yet this time, pulled and sustained by the thread of magic linking her to her mother, driven by fear and anger and love and despair, and powered by the shard in her hand, the journey seemed to take no time at all.

Perhaps, she thought later, the time taken by all her previous journeys had been self-imposed: her rational mind trying to make sense of the non-rational abilities she had inherited from the Lady. After all, her body did not *literally* dissolve into water or mist and then reassemble itself. The water, the clouds, were mere conduits for her magical power. The real journey happened at the speed of thought, and if she got out of her own mind's way, that was a very fast speed indeed.

But she was thinking none of that now, as she rushed

to her mother's aid. All she knew was that she had to reach her mother immediately – and immediately, she was *there*, above Vancouver Island, still gripped in mist and cloud.

But mist and cloud did not allow her to materialize: the restriction on her power that required her to reassemble in water deep enough to submerge her body remained. She found the nearest body of water, a tiny pond in the woods, and exploded out of it.

She could sense her mother just a few hundred metres away. She still held the shard of Excalibur in her hand: she peeled down the top of her swimsuit and tucked the shard back inside the tensor bandage she always wore around her waist. She pulled up the swimsuit again and set off barefoot through the trees, the power within her flinging the tiny droplets of mist away from her skin, keeping her dry though it could not keep her warm. But she gave the chill no thought, no more than she gave to the branches lashing at her bare skin or the wet leaves squishing between her toes.

She reached the edge of the trees, and found herself looking out at a rustic campground, a main building of peeled logs next to an unpaved parking lot, smaller cabins peeking out from the trees on the far side of the clearing.

The parking lot held a single vehicle: a black SUV with the Excalibur Computer Systems logo on the door.

Mom was in the main building. Ariane didn't have to guess, she *knew*. She could feel her there, the thread of power she had followed and drawn on now the equivalent of a thick, steel cable linking them. Raw anger raged within her. Rex Major had *threatened her mother*. The men inside had kidnapped her from her job, were holding her hostage to force her to give up the shards of Excalibur she had already gathered, the shards that were rightfully hers as the Lady of the Lake – hers and her mother's, for the Lady's blood flowed in them both.

Her mother might not be able to use the power within her, but it was still there, and through the connection Ariane had forged with her mom when at last she had found her, Ariane could draw on that power as well as her own, use her mother's power as well as the shard's to supplement her own flagging energy.

The drizzle pattered down around her. Ariane spread her hands and gathered the water together, from out of the air and up from the wet ground.

A puddle formed in front of her, grew to become a pool. It heaved up in the middle until it was as tall as she was, and then taller; as thick as she was, and then thicker. With fury and power blazing in her mind, she shaped it into a water-woman, a shimmering, living humanoid shape, like the one the Lady had manifested as when Ariane and Wally had met her in the chamber beneath Wascana Lake.

The still-falling rain bounced off of the water-woman as though she were made of glass or diamond. Ariane sat down cross-legged on the wet grass, closed her eyes, and threw her consciousness into her new body.

Suddenly she was taller, and stronger, and no longer felt the cold, even distantly. The thread of power from her mother continued to pull on her, even in this new body. She stalked forward. The door might or might not have been locked: it didn't matter. She drew back her water-heavy arm and punched, and the door smashed inward, the doorframe shattering with the force of the blow. She half-dissolved, flowed into the room beyond, the camp kitchen, then reformed her shape.

Two big men in dark suits stood on either side of her mother, who was tied to a wooden chair. Her eyes were wide and white and frightened above the duct-tape gagging her, but no wider or whiter or more frightened than those of the men, who fumbled for shoulder holsters, swearing.

Guns blazed. Bullets slashed through Ariane's water-body, shattered the windows behind her, tore chunks from the log walls.

She took five steps forward, and tossed the men aside.

The one to the left hit the legs of a heavy wooden worktable. They broke in two, and the tabletop thudded down on top of him. The one to the right hit the stove so hard he dented the door and smashed the tempered-glass window.

Neither of them moved after that.

Water-Ariane looked down at her mother, saw her mother's terror, and let her body dissolve. Real Ariane scrambled to her feet and ran into the building, splashing and skidding through the puddles her water-body had left on the linoleum. She pulled the gag from her mother's mouth.

"Ariane?" Emily Forsythe gasped. "I knew you were coming. I told myself it was just wishful thinking, but I *knew*...I could feel it."

Ariane struggled to untie the knots holding her mom to the chair. "We have to get out of here," she said. Suddenly she hesitated. "I'm still carrying one of the shards," she said. "The last time I got close with one..."

"I can...feel it," her mom said. "But it's not like before."

Ariane wondered what that meant, but now wasn't the time to worry about it. The knots came loose at last. Her mom was free.

The man under the table groaned, and the tabletop moved. Ariane grabbed Mom's hand, ran out into the rain, and let the clouds take them away.

◄► ►

Enraged, momentarily helpless, and in serious danger of being pulled under by his clothing, Rex Major floundered in the water. As he finally struggled over to the ladder and began hauling himself dripping up to the top of the platform again, he saw Wally clambering up the slippery boulders at the base of the cataract, making his escape through the cavern's natural entrance. Major swore, turned, and shouted down at Felicia, who was treading water in the middle of the pool, "Get out and get after him!"

"I can't!" Felicia shouted.

"Why not?" What on earth was wrong with the girl?

"Because when Wally grabbed the shard it cut the waist band of my bikini bottom."

"So?"

"So I'm practically naked!" The girl sounded as furious as he was. "Half my swimsuit is on the bottom of the pool!"

"You think I care about that?" Merlin roared at her. "Get after him!"

"I care," Felicia shouted back. "I'm not getting out while you're there."

Merlin swore again, spun around, spotted the towel Felicia had dropped on the platform before she had jumped into the pool, and kicked it to the top of the ladder. "Get out, grab the towel, follow me," he ordered, then turned and ran for the stairs.

The storm that had threatened as he and Felicia made their way to the cavern along the shore path had broken in earnest. Lightning and thunder played cat-and-mouse across the black sky and the rain fell in such torrents he felt half under water again. He ran across the wooden bridge that spanned the cataract just above the cave mouth, and then to the bottom of the path leading up to Lake Tanama, where at once a flash of lightning showed him Wally, climbing. The first part of the path was exposed, but within minutes the boy would be under the trees and lost to sight – and Merlin *needed* him in sight.

Wally had the shard, and Merlin would not let him get away with it.

He turned his head. Where was the blasted girl? In another flash of lightning he saw Felicia picking her way toward him, towel tied around her hips. "Hurry!" he shouted at her.

She reached him a minute later and stared up into the rain. "What's Wally doing?"

"Trying to get away with the fourth shard," Merlin growled. "And failing." He pulled the second shard from his pocket and held it out. "Grab hold."

Felicia took it.

Instantly the tiny thread of power that ran from Faerie to Merlin thickened, filling Merlin with more magic than he had had in a very long time: still the merest shadow of the power he had once enjoyed, a flickering candle compared to the conflagration of his former sorcerous strength, but enough.

Once he could have summoned a storm such as the one that howled above Cacibajagua Island at will, and hurled it against his – and Arthur's – enemies. That power still eluded him, but with the storm already in place, with the electricity leaping like startled deer from cloud to cloud and from cloud to ground, and with his knowledge of the True Name of lightning, he did not need all the power he'd once owned. He needed only the power that was his, here and now, thanks to the one shard he carried, and the touch of Arthur's heir upon the blade, to do...

...this!

The bolt of lightning Major summoned didn't strike Wally directly: not because Rex Major any longer cared what happened to the boy, but only because he did not know what that much power would do to the precious shard Wally carried. Instead, the lightning struck the trail just above Wally, the eye-searing flash burning a purple path through Major's eyesight, the crack of thunder striking him with physical force. Flish gasped and let go of her end of the shard, cutting him off from the bulk of his power, but the lightning had done its work: Wally, hurled through the air by the explosive force of the strike, tumbled backward down the slope and thudded to a crumpled, motionless heap, water sluicing around his pale body, blood running from a wound in his shoulder, the fourth shard of Excalibur lying just centimetres from his slack, outstretched hand.

"You've killed him!" Flish screamed.

"Probably not," Merlin growled, "but even if I have, it's no more than he deserved."

"You –"

"Quiet!" Merlin roared the word, and enough power remained in him that his voice, in that moment, was louder than the storm. He could not Command Felicia, but she was only a girl and he *could* cow her. She stumbled back from him, hands over her ears, as he turned and splashed up the path to Wally's motionless form. He snatched up the shard and, without a second glance at the boy, returned to the path that led back to the resort...and his private jet, fuelled and awaiting his return.

"Follow me," he ordered Felicia.

"What about Wally?" she said. She stared up at her brother, her face pale in the almost-continuous flashes of lightning. "He's my brother..."

"He belongs to the Lady of the Lake," Merlin snarled. "Let her look after him." He grabbed Felicia's wrist, and she grabbed her soaking-wet towel as it threatened to slip off. "We're leaving. Now."

Two shards on his person, and Ariane's mother his hostage: he would soon have the entire blade, and with that in his possession, and much of his power returned, finding the hilt would be a simple matter.

By summer the sword Excalibur would be complete and in his grasp, and the subjugation of Earth – and subsequent liberation of Faerie – could finally begin.

"Walk faster," he snapped at Felicia. "We're going home."

She said something but he paid no attention, just kept his grip upon her arm and strode through the wind and rain. *Toward victory,* he told himself.

CHAPTER SEVENTEEN

VOWS OF VENGEANCE

ARIANE MATERIALIZED WITH HER MOTHER in the pool at the bottom of the Medicine Hat Lodge waterslide without regard for the startlement of anyone who might be present. Once again the transition had been almost instantaneous: Her subconscious – or the Lady's magic – somehow finding the route through cloud and stream and pipe to her chosen destination without her having to consciously think about it, as she always had before.

She, at least, was wearing a swimsuit, whereas her mom still wore her Empress Tea Lobby uniform of slacks and vest and long-sleeved white shirt. But people didn't linger at the bottom of the waterslide, and they'd lucked out: no one was actually in that part of the pool at the moment, though Ariane could hear children shouting somewhere up above her. She guided her mom to the edge. Her mother, clearly shaken and bewildered, moved almost mechanically, climbing out onto her hands and knees just as a boy shot off the end of the waterslide and splashed into the pool behind them. He surfaced, spluttering, and gave Ariane and her mom a startled look.

"She fell in," Ariane said, smiling brightly. "Nothing

to worry about."

The boy nodded, wide-eyed, and then hurried to the other side of the pool to make his own exit as a little girl came squealing down the slide.

Ariane clambered out herself, took hold of her mom's arm, and ordered the water off of both of them. Dry again, and arm in arm, they walked the length of the pool to the lobby, and from there to Emma's room.

Emma had promised to stay at the hotel until she heard from Ariane and Wally, and although to Ariane it seemed weeks since she had made that promise, it had actually only been the day before. Emma answered the door at the first knock, and her eyes widened as she saw who stood there.

"Emma, this is my mom, Emily Forsythe," Ariane said. "Mom, this is Emma Macphail."

"Hi," Mom said. Then she burst into tears.

Emma stood aside as Ariane guided her mother into the room. Mom sat at the end of the bed. Emma sat beside her and put her arms around her while she wept as if she would never stop. Emma looked up at Ariane. "What happened?"

"A lot," Ariane said. She hated to see her mother cry, but she didn't have time for this. "I have to go."

She turned toward the bathroom.

"*What?*" Emma cried.

"Ariane, no!" her mom called after her. "Please, I need you...we have to..."

Ariane turned around. The shard of Excalibur at her side burned, a spark lighting her anger, and she did nothing to control it. "I've needed you for *two years*, Mom," she almost snarled. "You're safe. Wally isn't. You can wait. He can't." She stepped into the bathroom, started the water running, paused to check her energy level. Minutes before, she'd been in the Caribbean, exhausted by her efforts to free the fourth shard. Then she'd recharged by her connection to her mother – and that energy was still with her.

"Ariane, I'm –" she heard her mother begin, and then she was gone.

Wally will be all right, she told herself, in the brief minutes she was without her body, all the time it took now for her to streak back to Cacibajagua Island. *He's smart. He can take care of himself.*

She burst out of the water of Lake Tanama in the middle of a howling storm. Lightning tore the clouds and thunder assaulted her ears. She scrambled out of the lake and stood on the path bordering it in the wind-whipped rain.

Realization hit her like a blow.

Rex Major – Merlin – had the fourth shard. She knew it from the altered song of the first shard at her side. She couldn't sense where he was, but he had to be heading back to the resort. She had to go after –

No. She had to find Wally.

She ran along the path around the lake to where it began its descent to the seashore. Water sluiced around her bare feet as she started down. The rain had made the path slippery as ice, but she ordered the water away from her feet so the ground turned bone-dry, and hurried down as sure-footed as a mountain goat.

The storm never eased. The wind tore through the palm fronds and bushes, bits of greenery flying across the path, vines whipping at her bare legs and arms and face. The lightning and thunder attacked the island like an endless artillery barrage.

And Ariane came out from under the trees and saw, in the flare of lightning, Wally lying unconscious on the path below her, his pale body, clad only in his swim trunks, sprawled awkwardly in the mud, the wound in his shoulder bleeding again.

Ariane's heart stuttered. "Wally!" she screamed. He didn't move.

Abandoning caution, she started to run down the path. Her feet slipped and she fell, rolled, brought up against a rock, stumbled up and continued running. She reached Wally and dropped to her knees beside him.

To her unutterable relief, she saw that he was breathing. His head lay against a rock. Had he hit it? She didn't see any blood from his head, only from his shoulder.

Was it safe to move him?

She stared around. There was no one in sight. She could take him to the resort, get them to –

No. Rex Major was there. She couldn't take a wounded Wally there and hand Major yet another hostage.

There was only one place she and Wally could go to get help.

She sat in the mud beside him, pulled his wet body close to hers, and took both of them north.

From the warm sluicing water of the rain-soaked Caribbean island to the chlorine-tinged water of the Medicine Hat Lodge pool took only moments. Ariane moved fast the moment they emerged beneath the waterslide, hauling Wally to the edge of the pool, keeping his head above water, and screaming, "Help! Help! He's hit his head! He's bleeding!"

A flurry of activity. Staff came running. People shouted questions. Ariane just kept saying, "He hit his head, he hit his head," and "Get my aunt, Room 211!"

Someone called 911. Emma appeared. "Ariane, what...?" she said.

"He hit his head," was all she said.

And all the time she held Wally, her arms beneath his arms, circling his chest, her body pressed up against his. She could feel him breathing, could feel his heart beating, but he still hadn't woken up...

The ambulance crew arrived. Ariane relinquished Wally at last, watched the crew immobilize his neck and head, dress the wound on his shoulder, ease him onto a backboard, place him on a gurney, roll him out. "I'm coming, too," she said.

"Ariane," Emma said. "You're only wearing your swimsuit. It's December."

"I don't care. I'm going in the ambulance."

"Your mother –"

"I'm going with Wally!" Ariane almost shouted at her. She found her fists clenched, loosened them. "It's my fault he got hurt. My fault he got involved in this at all. And then I left him to Rex Major...I'm going with him. I'm not leaving him until I know he's all right."

Emma stared at her then nodded, once. "All right, Ariane," she said. "I'll bring some clothes to the hospital. Go."

Ariane turned without another word and hurried after the paramedics.

Please let him be all right, she whispered. She'd never gone to church, and prayer wasn't something that came naturally to her, but all the same, this wasn't the first time she'd prayed – that had been when her mother had disappeared.

Please let him be all right.

And then the shard burned against her side, and she added, *And if he isn't, Rex Major will pay...Rex Major and Felicia Knight.*

Wally's sister had helped Merlin get the fourth shard. She must have known Wally was hurt, must have known Merlin had left him lying in the mud on that steep hillside path, and had done *nothing*. If they'd been able to take off in the storm, they'd be in the air by now, flying back to Toronto, flying back to the lifestyles-of-the-rich-and-famous luxury that was all Flish cared about. She'd left her brother in the mud, dying – or already *dead* for all she knew – just so she could get back to her big-screen media room.

Ariane had hurt Flish badly once before, breaking her leg in the confrontation on the tennis court between her and the coven of mean girls of which Flish had been a part. Wally had been horrified. It had opened the gulf between them into which Rex Major had driven his wedge of lies and half-truths. Ariane had apologized, had promised Wally, for his sake, that she wouldn't hurt Flish again...

...but it was a promise she would break in an instant if Wally were seriously hurt, and Flish had had anything to do with it.

And as for Rex Major...

The sword kept telling her to kill her enemies, to use its power to strike them down.

For the first time, she thought it might have a point worth listening to.

She clambered into the back of the ambulance, took Wally's hand, and rode with him to the hospital, staring down at his white face, but thinking black, black thoughts.

◄ ►

The storm began to die away as Major and Felicia hurried along the path to the resort, though even after the rain eased the massive waves crashing against the rocks to their left doused them with salt spray. Their route took them into a lush tropical garden at the back of the rambling two-storey structure. Calling it a hotel was over-praising it, Major thought; it boasted only forty rooms. But then, cave diving wasn't for everyone. Those who came to dive Joju Cave – and the others on the island, many of which were far more technically challenging and dangerous – were willing to pay a premium for the adventure.

Well, he wouldn't have to spend another night there. "The storm has eased enough we should be able to take off," he said to Flish as they entered the garden. "I'll have my pilot prepare the plane. Go to your room and put on some clothes."

But Flish stopped at the garden's wrought-iron gate, hung on two stone pillars topped with gas torches that flickered and flared in what was now a mere drizzle and a fitful breeze. "No," she said.

"No?" Major said. "You'd prefer to fly naked?"

"No," Felicia said. "I'm not going anywhere until you send someone back for Wally. You can't just leave him lying there."

Major felt anger boil up in him. He knew – because he knew the ways of Excalibur so well – that some of it was coming from the two shards of Excalibur he now bore, even if he could not access their power without Felicia's Arthur-empowered touch. But much of it – maybe most of it – was his own. He was utterly and completely fed up with the interfering troublesome teenagers that had plagued his life since his cursed sister had managed to convince Ariane Forsythe to accept the power of the Lady of the Lake.

"I told you," he snarled, "that he's the Lady's problem – Ariane's problem. He could have worked with me, he could have been at my side when we came here to retrieve the fourth shard instead of you, but he betrayed me, attacked my men, and stole the third shard when it was in my grasp. I will not lift a finger to help him."

"Then I will," Felicia said. She suddenly darted past him, holding her towel in place with one hand while she cupped the other to her mouth to shout, "Help! Help! Someone's hurt!"

"Oh, *for God's sake!*" Merlin roared. He could not

Command Felicia, but he had other powers even without her touching the shard: the mere fact four of them were now at loose in the world had strengthened the thread of magic from Faerie. He clenched his fist and the path in front of her heaved, throwing her as if it were a bucking bronco. She fell hard, losing the towel in the process, and scrambled for it to cover herself again as Major strode toward her. "Very well!" he said as he glared down at her. "I will have the resort staff go to your brother. But we will not wait for him to be returned here. We will fly away as soon as the plane is ready. *Now* will you get dressed?"

Felicia gathered the towel around her and stood up, tying it again at her back. "All right," she said. Her face was red, though whether with embarrassment or anger he couldn't tell. "But I want proof they're going after Wally before I get on the plane."

"I'll give it to you right now," Merlin said. "Come inside."

He stalked along the path through the remainder of the garden, brushing aside the giant flowers hanging low, weighed down by the rainfall, his feet crushing the petals the rain had driven from some of them. He walked into the lobby, made to look like the inside of a tropical hut, all wooden beams and bamboo and palm fronds. Peter Camus came out from the office behind the desk as they entered.

"Are you all right?" he said anxiously. "We were worried. The storm came up so suddenly. Lewis staggered back some time ago but he seemed very confused, and couldn't tell us anything about what had happened to the two of you. He was bleeding – I think maybe he fell and hit his head. Did you shelter in the cave?" His gaze flicked to Felicia, in her skimpy blue bikini top and mud-stained towel, and she looked down, flushing.

Major could imagine what Camus thought. He also didn't care. "In a manner of speaking. There has been considerable damage in the cave...a lightning strike shattered some of the rocks. And there was a boy – one of those two shipwrecked teens Lewis found in the hut. We saw him on the path up to the lake, then there was another lightning strike, and we couldn't see him anymore. We didn't dare look for him, with the storm, and poor Felicia...we thought it best to get back to the resort as quickly as we could. But you should send someone out immediately to look for him, and the girl, too, to make certain they're all right."

"At once!" Camus said. He ran back into the office and Merlin could hear him talking on the phone, though he couldn't make out the words. A few minutes later he returned. "I've got a couple of men heading out there now with a first-aid kit and a stretcher. If the boy is injured, we'll find him and bring him back."

"I'm glad to hear it," Major said. He gave Felicia a pointed look. "Aren't *you* glad to hear it?"

"Very glad," Felicia muttered. "Can I go get dressed now?"

"I think you should," Major said. "We'll be leaving within the hour."

Felicia hurried out of the lobby. Camus watched her go then swung his gaze back to Merlin. "Leaving, Mr. Major?"

"Yes," Major said. And then he switched to the Voice of Command. "Call your men. Tell them to come back. There is no boy."

"Of course, Mr. Major." Camus went back into the office again, gave new orders, came out again. "Leaving, Mr. Major?" he repeated, as if the previous few moments had never happened – which, in his mind, they hadn't.

"Yes," Merlin said again. "Please have the driver come around to take us to the airstrip. Thank you for your hospitality. It has been an enlightening and profitable visit. I will speak to your owner about a possible investment."

"Wonderful news, Mr. Major!" Camus said. "Thank you so much for coming."

"It has been," Rex Major said, "entirely my pleasure."

He left the lobby for his own room. He'd packed his suitcase before he'd headed back to the cave, in expectation he would want to leave the moment he returned to the resort. He kept the shards of Excalibur on his person – he'd had a bad experience with a previous attempt to tuck a shard away in a suitcase, even with a protective spell – and took his suitcase down to the lobby. Felicia, now fully dressed, awaited him there. Silently they climbed into the overgrown golf cart that would take them to the airstrip. As they rode, Major checked his email on his phone...and swore, a single obscene word fired from his lips like a bullet.

"What now?" Felicia said.

"That brat Ariane Forsythe managed to rescue her mother," he snarled. "I don't even know how she found her. Or how she got there that fast." He stopped, thought, and then swore again as he understood what it had to mean. "She's growing in power, just as I am. She's gaining more of my *dear* sister's abilities, the powers she would have taught Ariane how to use if I hadn't forced her out of the world as quickly as I did."

He pulled the fourth shard of Excalibur out of his pocket. "We each have two shards," he said. He wasn't really talking to Felicia, but to himself. "We each have an heir of Arthur to help us draw on their power." He tightened his fist on the shard, just shy of the point where the blade would cut into his flesh. "Stalemate."

"There's one more piece to go, isn't there?" Felicia said.

Merlin nodded. They'd reached the airstrip, and the ride had smoothed as the cart moved from the gravel road to the resort onto the smooth tarmac of the strip. At the end, Merlin's jet waited, the hatch open, a warm, welcoming light spilling down the steps.

"The hilt," he said. "Whoever gets it will be able to command the other to give up their shards voluntarily – and Excalibur will be reforged and whole once more." He rubbed the ruby stud in his ear. "Almost."

"Reforged how?" Felicia said. "Hard to find a sword-smith these days."

"The sword will forge itself," Merlin said. He put the shard back into his pocket. "Neither of us will be able to sense the final piece while the other holds two shards. But it will reveal itself to me, just as this shard did." He patted his pocket. "All it takes is one smartphone to get close enough to the hilt's hiding place for the magic I have wound into the Internet to detect it. Ariane does not have that ability. She will not interfere again."

"Isn't that what you said this time?" Felicia said, and then turned her gaze once more to the private jet as the cart's driver delivered them to the foldaway staircase that descended from the airplane's open hatch. The pilot came down the steps to carry their luggage aboard for them.

Major was about to give a short, sharp answer to her impertinent question when the sight of the pilot reminded him of another issue. They climbed aboard and the pilot sealed the hatch. But when the girl went to strap herself in, Major stopped the man before he could go into the cockpit.

"I have a question," he said.

"Yes, sir?"

"If someone wanted to know where this plane is going, is there a way they could find out?"

The pilot thought for no more than a second before saying, "Well, of course I have to file a flight plan specifying our destination."

Major felt a chill. "Is that a public document?"

"Yes, sir. It's available on the Internet."

"Ah, thank you. Let's get underway."

"Yes, sir." The pilot went into the cockpit. Major joined Felicia in the forward lounge and buckled in. He schooled his face to impassiveness, but inside he was seething. *All those layers of security, and I left a back door wide open. A door I didn't even know existed. And that meddlesome brat walked right through it. Twice! Laughing at me!*

The jet's engines cycled up. They began to move. Major's thoughts went to another meddlesome teenager.

Ariane Forsythe will not interfere again, he told himself. *She must have left a trail, rescuing her mother. I'll put more men on the case. I'll find her. I can't kill her – not yet – but I'll put a stop to her interference once and for all.*

Once. And. For. All.

The thought accompanied him all the way back to Toronto. It wasn't a threat.

It was a promise.

CHAPTER EIGHTEEN

"GOD BLESS US, EVERY ONE!"

WALLY WOKE. He blinked up at speckled acoustic tiles, a curtain hanging from a metal track, a susurration of voices, public-address announcements, machines beeping...

Hospital. He reached up and touched his head. It wasn't bandaged, which was something, but it still hurt. So did his bruised and lacerated shoulder.

Great, he thought. *Probably another concussion. At last I'll have something in common with my hockey-playing friends.*

Well, I would if I had any.

What had happened? He remembered Major showing up in the cave. He remembered clambering over Ariane, then – holy mackerel! He'd been *shot* at by Jacob Lewis!

Now he remembered jumping into the water, grabbing the shard off Flish, climbing up toward the lake...

But after that, everything was a blank.

Major, he thought. *He must have done something.* But clearly it hadn't been enough to stop Wally Knight. He felt pretty good, actually, all things considered. Except for the headache and the shoulder ache. And the hunger. When had he last eaten?

He felt a pricking in his left wrist and looked down. An IV line snaked into it, held in place by white surgical tape. He didn't like the sight of metal piercing his flesh, so he looked the other way instead – just in time to see Ariane push aside the privacy curtain.

Her eyes were red. She'd been crying. *Over me?* he thought, and felt a wave of tenderness and affection. "Hi," he said.

She gasped, and then flung herself at him. "You're all right!"

She was hurting his shoulder but he didn't mind a bit. "Well," he said, his voice muffled by her head, which, pressed to his chest, made it hard to open his jaw. Her hair smelled like flowers. "I guess so."

She drew back, brushed the hair out of her eyes, and then kissed him on the mouth for...

Well, he wasn't sure how long, since his brain suddenly seemed to not be working again, even though he was fully conscious, but it was definitely a long time. A *good*, long time. A freaking *excellently* long time...

When she drew back, he gulped air, then said, "Wow."

"You've been unconscious for a whole day," she said. "I was so worried – the doctor said he couldn't find anything wrong with you, but you wouldn't wake up."

"Nothing wrong with me?" Wally touched his head again. "My head hurts. Isn't it a concussion?"

"The doctor didn't think so."

"Then what...?"

"Rex Major," Ariane said. "Merlin. He did something. Knocked you out somehow. And then he –"

"Stole the shard." Wally closed his eyes, feeling sick in a way that had nothing to do with whatever had put him in the hospital. "Ariane, I'm so sorry. I tried –"

"Don't you dare apologize, Wally Knight," Ariane snapped. "I'm the one who should be apologizing. For getting you involved. For abandoning you at the cave. For –"

"I involved myself," Wally said. "I *wanted* to be involved. And I abandoned you first. I left you to face Major. I thought if I could get out, hide, I could come back later and do something to help. And I tried. I knocked Major into the water, jumped in, wrestled with Felicia, got the shard, ran out again. Major came after me, and I remember seeing Felicia wearing a towel around her waist..." He frowned. "I wonder why? Anyway, that's the last thing I remember."

"I found you on the path up to Lake Tanama," Ariane said. "When I came back from rescuing my mother."

Wally blinked. "You rescued your mom?"

"Major's men kidnapped her from the Empress. They were holding her at some kind of camp in the woods. But I could *feel* her, Wally, like I can feel the sword – like *you* can feel the sword. I had a magical connection. I followed it."

"But it should have taken you hours to –"

Ariane shook her head. "It didn't. It *doesn't,* anymore. I think that was just a...mental block on my part. Why should it take that long? Why should it take any time at all? It's *magic.* I reached Vancouver Island in *minutes,* got Mom to Medicine Hat and handed her over to Emma in minutes, and got back to the island in *minutes.* But it was still too long. Major was gone, Felicia was gone, I thought you were dead. I transported you back to Medicine Hat, and they called 911."

"So this is Medicine Hat?" Wally said, staring up at the acoustic tile.

Ariane nodded.

And then Wally suddenly sat up. The motion brought a sharp pain to his head, but he ignored it. "Wait! They will have admitted me...using a computer."

"Yes, but –"

"Major will find out I'm here!"

"He left you for dead. He won't even be looking!" Ariane protested.

Wally shook his head. *"No.* He left me for *you.* If I died, fine. But if you found me, he knew you'd have to take me somewhere for medical attention. He'll have his feelers out through all the networks his software has infiltrated – and it's *everywhere.* My admittance will have raised a red flag."

"They can't grab you out of the hospital," Ariane protested.

"They grabbed your mother out of the Empress," Wally pointed out. "If Merlin Commanded them to do so – and he will have – they'll do whatever it takes to grab me. Including hurting other people." He pulled the tape from his wrist, yanked out the IV drip, wincing as he did so.

"Wally!" Ariane said. "You can't –"

"He's in here, doctor," a voice was saying in the hall. "A fascinating patient. We can't find anything wrong with him, but he's unconscious. All tests have been negative. It's very kind of you to fly in from Toronto just to take a look. May I ask how you found out about the case?"

"You could say a little birdie told me," said a deep voice, and Wally's eyes jerked wide. He knew that voice.

Emeka! He should have still been in the hospital from his own head injury, but there he was, outside, in the hall, *now!*

"We have to go," he whispered frantically to Ariane. He swung his bare feet over the side of the bed. He was wearing a hospital gown over hospital-issued pajama bottoms. "Hurry!"

Ariane, after one horrified glance at the door, didn't hesitate. She took his hand, pulled him into the en-suite bathroom, and locked the door. She turned on the tap. "Hang on –"

Whirling nothingness, but very, very short this time.

Wally barely had time to register how disturbing the process was before he was coughing and spitting chlorinated water.

The Medicine Hat Lodge waterslide pool. Again.

But dark and empty, shut down for the night. For once they wouldn't face any startled looks. He climbed out, the thin hospital clothing clinging to him like a second skin. Ariane ordered the water off of both of them, and then they hurried through the hotel to Emma's room, the one she'd been sharing with Ariane. Ariane's mother sat in one of the chairs by the round table, gazing out the window. Emma was reclining on the bed, propped up by pillows, reading a book. Both of them looked toward the door as it opened. "Wally?" Emma said. "What –"

"We have to go. Now!" Ariane said. "Get packed."

"What's happened?" Ariane's mother said.

"Rex Major's man, Emeka," Wally said. "At the hospital. We got out the...usual way." He nodded at Ariane. "But he'll be here next – they'll know I was brought to the hospital from the waterslide. Major may already have someone watching the hotel. We have to get out of town and get back to Barringer Farm without being followed."

Emma had already put down her book and stood up. She stared narrowly at Wally. "Are you sure you're all right? You were unconscious –"

"I'm all right." In truth, his head hurt worse than ever and the way his stomach felt he was glad he hadn't eaten anything recently.

Grown-ups, in Wally's experience, were maddeningly slow when leaving a hotel room – you threw your stuff into a suitcase, you headed out the door, what could possibly take so long? – but Emma and Ariane's mother moved remarkably quickly for their ages. Wally couldn't help noticing how little Ariane said to her mother, and wondered what *that* was all about: she'd been looking for her mom for two years and already she was doing the tetchy teen-girl-with-her-mother thing he'd seen Felicia go through for years.

Well, they could sort it out at Barringer Farm. First they had to get there.

Fifteen minutes after Wally and Ariane reached the hotel room they were all heading down the hall. In the lobby, Emma stopped to check out. Late afternoon was an unusual time to do so, but Emma paid the one-day penalty she had to swallow without complaint, and the four of them hurried to the lobby doors.

A big black SUV had just pulled up outside under the overhang.

Golden letters on the door read, "Excalibur Computer Systems."

"Crap," Wally said.

◄◄ ►►

Ariane had been overjoyed when Wally woke up, horrified when Emeka had shown up outside his room, and in complete agreement they had to get out of the hotel at once.

She couldn't stand another night in there anyway, with her mother.

She'd been so happy to find her mom, so determined to save her when Rex Major had threatened her, but now that she had her close at hand, now that they had to start living together again...

Every time Ariane looked at her she thought of the night Mom had shown up wet and distraught on the doorstep, the horrible days when she'd been in the psych ward at the hospital, screaming whenever Ariane tried to visit her, insisting she didn't have a daughter, that she didn't know who Ariane was, every word a knife to Ariane's already scraped-raw heart. And then the worst blow of all: she'd disappeared, escaped somehow, taken all her money out of her account, in cash, and fled.

Aunt Phyllis had been all but convinced her sister was dead. Ariane had never believed it. She'd been sure her mother was still out there somehow, and that if only she could find her, they could go back to the happy life they'd had before the night the Lady of the Lake offered Ariane's mother her magical power – and her mother had rejected it.

But they couldn't go back, could they? She could never forget the hell her mother had put her through. And now that she was the Lady of the Lake, she had some measure of the Lady's contempt for the heir who had rejected her inheritance. If her mother had accepted the Lady's power, and the Lady's quest, she could have rounded up the shards of Excalibur before Rex Major could have even begun. He hadn't had the power then that he had now. His skein of magic hadn't yet been draped around the world via the Internet. The sword could have been quickly reforged, handed back to the true Lady of the Lake in Faerie, and the door between the worlds closed and sealed for good.

Ariane would never have known anything about it, unless her mother chose to tell her many years after the fact. She would have grown up as a normal teenager in a normal home, not bounced from foster home to foster home and school to school, bullied, an outcast, rarely finding friendship and never keeping it as she moved on yet again.

She had longed with all her heart for her mother to be returned to her. And now that her mother had been, she discovered she had very little to say to her.

Which was a particularly uncomfortable state of affairs when you were locked into the same hotel room, which was one reason Ariane was looking forward very much to returning to Barringer Farm.

But now here they were at the doors of the hotel – and Rex Major's men were pulling up outside.

She stared at the SUV, saw the faces of the men in it, and felt anger kindle inside of her, her own anger providing the initial spark, the shards fanning the flames. So often she'd tamped down that rage, afraid of what she would do if she gave into it.

This time she did not.

"All right," she said, under her breath. "You want trouble? I'll give you trouble."

The Lady's power roared up inside her. Her senses expanded. She reached out through the magic, seeking water – and found it.

The heavy snow had collected on the flat roof that sheltered the front entrance of the hotel: collected, and melted, forming puddles beneath ice and more snow. There wasn't a lot of water...but there was enough.

The lobby faded around her as she reached out with the power, took hold of the water, and turned it into a weapon. She drove it down through stone and wood and metal, spread it out, turned some of it to ice, and then pulled...

...and just as the doors of the SUV opened and two men started to get out, the roof above them collapsed.

The deluge of debris poured down around them, burying the vehicle, crushing its roof, smashing in the hood, shattering the windows. After a moment's shocked silence in the lobby, people started screaming, hotel staff ran for the doors, someone was shouting into a phone.

"Wow," Wally said.

Ariane turned her back on what she had just done. "We'll use another door," she said.

"Ariane –" Her mother whispered.

"Now!" Ariane snapped the word with all the force of the anger that still filled her, and her mother, Emma, and Wally followed her along one of the ground-floor corridors to another exit, and then out into the snowy parking lot. They piled into the Ford Explorer. Emma started the engine as, with sirens blaring and lights flashing, a police cruiser, a fire truck and an ambulance poured into the parking lot. Emma put the vehicle in gear and they drove out.

Ariane found herself shaking, still filled with rage and power. Wally, beside her in the back seat, put out his hand and touched hers. "Ariane," he whispered. "Come back."

And suddenly the rage drained away. She let the Lady's power subside, and she took his hand – then she turned to him and laid her head against his shoulder, sobbing.

He put his arm around her and ran his hand across her head. "We got away," he said softly "It's over. We escaped."

We escaped, Ariane thought, *but it's not over. Rex Major has two shards. I have two shards. He has Felicia. And I...* She pushed her head harder against Wally, like a cat rubbing up against a trusted human. *I have Wally.*

Now we have to find the hilt. And then, maybe, it will be over.

But what other horrible things will I have to do, what other horrible things will have to happen, before we reach that point?

She had no answer. She felt drained, now, drained of energy and emotion and everything else, and as the Explorer took them home, she kept her head on Wally's shoulder, and slept.

◄◄ ►►

Golden and steaming, smelling delicious, the turkey could have been a prop in a made-for-TV Christmas movie. Artfully arranged around it on the festive red tablecloth were dressing and cranberry sauce, mashed potatoes and gravy, buns and butter, glazed carrots, and (the only sour note as far as Wally was concerned), a bowl of brussels sprouts.

Bing Crosby crooned, "White Christmas" in the background, a fire crackled in the fireplace, and snow fell gently outside in big, fluffy flakes.

Wally sat next to Ariane on one side of the dining-room table at Barringer Farm, across from Ariane's mother and Aunt Phyllis. Wally grinned at both of them. The moment when Emily and Phyllis Forsythe had been reunited, that night Emma drove them all back from Medicine Hat Lodge, had been one of the happiest things he had ever seen.

Emma herself sat at the head of the table. In addition to all her other skills, she'd proved to be a remarkable cook, and had taken charge of their Christmas dinner a week ago. Pumpkin pie and chocolate chip macaroons – Aunt Phyllis's contribution, much to Wally's delight – still awaited them, assuming they had any room left after this feast.

Holly hung from the beams of the dining-room ceiling, and in the living room, just visible to Wally through the archway to his right, the big Christmas tree glowed red and green and blue and yellow, close – but not *too* close – to the crackling fire in the giant hearth. Presents awaited their opening after dinner – a form of delayed gratification Wally wasn't sure he entirely approved of – but, he told himself, when in Rome...

He smiled at Ariane, who smiled back. She'd become more like her old self in the past couple of weeks. Hearing on the news that the men in the SUV hadn't been seriously injured in the roof collapse she'd engineered had helped. So had knowing, through the Lady's power, that Merlin had not yet found the hilt of Excalibur. Apparently he was as unable to feel its location as she was.

But the biggest difference was that she'd finally had time to talk to her mother. Wally hadn't listened to those conversations, but Ariane had told him that she now realized her mother had only acted for her benefit: all that Emily Forsythe had done had been meant to protect her daughter.

"How can I blame her?" she'd told him one night as they'd cuddled on the couch in front of the fireplace in the living room. "It's not like I've made perfect decisions since I got caught up in this whole mess. She may even have been right. Rex Major might have kidnapped me the moment he found out I existed. In which case he might already have Excalibur and be working on taking over the world."

She and her mother seemed easier with each other, at any rate. Wally liked Emily Forsythe, and thought she liked him, and that made him happy.

He hadn't contacted his parents again; he didn't dare. He didn't know if they had the police looking for him. He assumed Rex Major continued to Command them not to worry about Felicia; he didn't know what Major had Commanded them regarding him.

He and Ariane would continue their home-schooling under Emma while they waited for the fifth and final piece of the sword to reveal itself. They'd remain at Barringer Farm, not even venturing as far as Maple Creek or Elkwater. As long as they remained hidden away, off the grid, Rex Major could not find them.

For the time being they were safe, they were warm – and they were about to be well fed.

Ariane's hand found his knee under the table. Wally covered it with his own, and gave her a grin.

It couldn't last. Eventually the last piece of Excalibur would reveal itself, either to them or to Rex Major, and the final confrontation would have to take place. Both Ariane and Major had greater power than ever before. When they faced each other again, who knew what cataclysmic forces would be unleashed?

Magical combat, danger, terror, and pain – all of it was coming. It could not be avoided.

But it wasn't here yet. Today was Christmas. Today, he was with friends. Today, there was peace on Earth. Peace – and an absolutely amazing feast. He reached out and picked up his glass of ginger ale, and held it up. "Merry Christmas!" he said. "God bless us, every one."

Ariane squeezed his knee with her right hand, and lifted her own glass with her left. "Merry Christmas," she said.

"Merry Christmas!" "Merry Christmas!" "Merry Christmas!" echoed the others.

They drank and put down their glasses, and then Emma reached for the carving knife and fork. "White meat or dark?" she said to Wally.

"Both!" he said.

And the feast began.

THE END

ACKNOWLEDGEMENTS

Thanks first to my terrific editor, Matthew Hughes – who, by the way, is himself a fabulous science fiction and fantasy author. You should read his stuff: www.archonate.com.

Second, thanks to the wonderful folks at Coteau Books for doing such a great job with design, publicity, and promotion. You're the best!

And third, thanks to my wife, Margaret Anne, and daughter, Alice (to both of whom I read this entire book aloud), for being loving, supporting…and putting up with a husband and father who spends his days making up stories.

ABOUT THE AUTHOR

EDWARD WILLETT is the award-winning author of more than fifty science-fiction and fantasy novels, science and other non-fiction books for both young readers and · adults, including the acclaimed fantasy series *The Masks of Aygrima*, written under the pen name E.C. Blake.

His science fiction novels include *Lost in Translation, Marseguro* and *Terra Insegura. Marseguro* won the 2009 Prix Aurora Award for best Canadian science-fiction or fantasy novel.

His non-fiction writing for young readers has received National Science Teachers Association and VOYA awards.

Edward Willett was born in New Mexico and grew up in Weyburn, Sask. He has lived and worked in Regina since 1988. In addition to his numerous writing projects, Edward is also a professional actor and singer who has performed in dozens of plays, musicals and operas in and around Saskatchewan, hosted local television programs and emceed numerous public events.